MAGIC AND MOLEMEN

Related titles by S. Usher Evans

PRINCESS VIGILANTE
The City of Veils
The Veil of Ashes
The Veil of Trust
The Queen of Veils

THE SEOD CROÍ CHRONICLES
A Quest of Blood and Stone
A Quest of Earth and Magic
A Quest of Sea and Soil
A Quest of Aether and Dust

THE MADION WAR TRILOGY
The Island
The Chasm
The Union

MAGIC AND MOLEMEN

Weary Dragon Inn

BOOK FIVE

S. Usher Evans

Sun's Golden Ray
Publishing

Pensacola, FL

Version Date: 2/27/24
© 2024 S. Usher Evans
ISBN: 978-1945438738

Map created by Luke Beaber of Stardust Book Services
Line Editing by Danielle Fine, By Definition Editing

Sun's Golden Ray Publishing
Pensacola, FL
www.sgr-pub.com

For ordering information, please visit
www.sgr-pub.com/orders

Dedication

To Merv's Fans

Town Hall
Witzel Butchery
Weary Dragon Inn
Town Squa[re]
Library
Mackey Bakery

ool
Pigsend Tea Shop
Flour Mill
Pigsend Village

Chapter One

"That thing has to be around here somewhere."

Bev wished she was scouring the small thicket near the Weary Dragon Inn for something mundane, like fresh spring blackberries for a delicious crisp. But, while there were blackberries to be found, mostly red and underripe, Bev was traipsing through the brush and bramble for something much more dangerous and potentially life-altering.

Biscuit, her trusty laelaps—a magical detection creature who resembled a small dog—had his nose to the ground, sniffing and pawing as he squeezed into spots too small for Bev to manage. Only the white tip of his tail was visible, his golden fur obscured by the thick vines and underbrush. Although Bev was doing her best to search, Biscuit would find what she was looking for much faster with that keen nose of his.

The laelaps let out a yelp of surprise, and a few moments later, reappeared in the clearing with half an engraved, wooden amulet in his mouth, tail wagging so fast it was hardly visible.

"Well done," Bev said, holding out the small basket she carried under her arm. "Put it here."

Biscuit deposited the amulet piece next to the other one he'd found a few minutes before. Bev held her breath, hoping they wouldn't glow or pop or do something *magical* when close to one another. But they just sat there, as dull and boring as a solstice ornament. It would've been easy to believe there was nothing special about them, but Bev knew differently. The last time she'd held them together, she'd been given a *terrible* vision about a battle she'd presumably been in, and more glimpses of a past she'd probably forgotten for a good reason.

"Okay, Biscuit," she said, covering the two pieces with the kitchen towel. "Let's head back to the inn. We've got chores to finish."

Biscuit trotted ahead of her as they left the thicket for the main road leading to the inn. Bev couldn't help but glance from side to side, searching the empty roads for a soldier. Of course, it was just after dawn, and there wasn't a soul stirring except for her and Biscuit. But one couldn't be too careful where the queen's soldiers were concerned.

It was because of one such soldier that Bev had even had the thought to retrieve the amulet pieces and investigate their mysterious origins further. She'd been content to live her life as the proprietor of the Weary Dragon Inn, a place she'd called home since arriving in Pigsend five years ago without a clue who she was or where she'd come from. But a magic-hunter named Dag Flanigan seemed convinced there was more to Bev than met the eye, and on his last visit to Pigsend had strongly insinuated he wanted to uncover the truth about her past.

Bev didn't think she had anything to hide, but the more visions she had, the more she worried Flanigan might just find something that would land her on the wrong side of the queen's laws. Which meant she had to retrieve the pieces of the only clue available to her and hope she could figure out the mystery before Flanigan did.

Not that Mr. Flanigan was nearby anymore. Last Bev knew, he was chasing dragons in the south, thanks to a clever diversion put on by a couple of local kids to keep him from capturing a *real* dragon shifter on the cusp of his first full transformation. Bev had almost completely forgotten about the broken amulet until she'd seen a similar one hanging from the neck of PJ Norris when he'd returned to town. She'd asked the elder dragon shifter, Rita, about it, and the lovely old woman had suggested Bev take the amulet pieces to someone who knew about magic.

Since the queen had seen to it that everything magical was destroyed, the only person Bev felt comfortable taking the amulet to was her friend Merv, a moleman who lived underground. He'd been an invaluable resource for many of the curiosities Bev had investigated recently, and if anyone would know something about the magical amulet, it was him.

But first, chores. She'd done as many as she could before the sun rose, but there were still a few left to get through. Her old mule Sin brayed from the stable as she and Biscuit returned to the back yard, perhaps complaining her breakfast had come much earlier than she'd wanted.

"So sorry, Your Majesty," Bev said, walking toward the kitchen door. "I'll be sure to feed you much later tomorrow."

She opened the kitchen door, holding it so Biscuit could come in, too, then headed straight for the kitchen table, placing the amulet basket underneath for safekeeping. On top, she had two large heaps of rosemary dough in bowls on the counter. One was made with her usual process—the same process that had earned her second place at last year's Harvest Festival. But the second...well, Bev was keen on winning first place this year.

She'd been tweaking something different every day in her tried and true recipe. Changing the amounts of all her ingredients, including the rosemary from her garden. Adding more time for the rise, the next day aiming for less. It was a slow, painstaking process, but her regular customers were more than happy to provide their opinions with each new batch.

Today, she was practicing a new technique where she simply added the ingredients together and let it sit for a while. The idea had come to her by accident yesterday. She'd mixed the flour, water, salt, rosemary, and barm together then got pulled away to deal with a guest who needed help with something. When she'd returned, the dough had completely changed in terms of texture. It was easier to knead, easier to assemble, and tasted pretty darn good, too.

Today, she was doing it intentionally. It had taken under an hour to find the amulet pieces, and while the dough was still dry on top, it was moist and stretchy underneath. Bev worked it, getting everything incorporated well then set it aside with a towel over it.

The rest of her chores couldn't be accomplished until her guests departed, so she walked out to the front room to tidy. She turned when Biscuit didn't follow her and found the laelaps sniffing at the basket under the table.

"Leave it alone," Bev warned, giving him a look.

He winced as if she'd struck him and came bounding over with his tongue unfurled over the side of his mouth.

"Mischievous little bugger."

The Weary Dragon was two stories, with seven bedrooms upstairs and a large front room that doubled as a dining room on the other side of the kitchen. Bev bustled around the room while she waited for her guests to come down, but just like Biscuit, her mind was on the amulet. If Merv didn't know anything about it, maybe she'd just leave it with him. It was probably safer away from Pigsend, anyway.

The front door opened, interrupting her thoughts, and Allen Mackey walked in carrying a basket of freshly baked muffins. The young baker, recently affianced, looked weary and drawn as he approached.

"Long night, Allen?" Bev asked, nodding appreciatively at the goods. "These look delightful."

"Vicky had me up until near midnight looking at wedding fabrics," he said with a loud yawn. "I told her I didn't care, that whatever made her happy made me happy, but she *insisted* on my input."

"Goodness. Well, be sure to grab a cup of tea from Etheldra when you head over that way," Bev said. "I hope tonight you can get some rest."

"Probably not. We're discussing the food tonight," he said with a grimace. "Not sure how we're going to feed all the people we've invited, but we'll do it."

"How many do you expect?" Bev had already blocked off the inn for their wedding weekend, leaving it available for Allen and Vicky's friends and family.

"Two hundred, maybe," he said. At Bev's horrified expression, he added, "Most of them are staying in Middleburg and coming to town for the wedding."

"Where are you going to be hosting it?" Bev asked.

"Mayor Hendry gave us the town hall," he said. "For a price, of course. Everything has a price. Did you know weddings are expensive? Thought I was going broke just buying her a ring."

Bev chuckled. "I can only imagine." She reached into her pocket and placed a gold coin on the counter. "For the cause. And the muffins."

Allen, usually one to decline payment, snatched the coin and stuffed it into his pocket. "I saw three upstairs, yeah?"

She nodded. "Seems to be the usual number these days. Steady business. That's what I like."

"I'm happy for you." He let out another yawn. "Suppose I should be getting the second batch over to Etheldra's."

The tea shop owner would certainly miss them if he didn't. "Well, try to get some rest today. We can't have you falling asleep in your sugar."

He left after that, and Bev couldn't help but feel for him. He really was trying to put on the best face possible for Vicky, but two hundred people? Bev couldn't even name two hundred people. There were maybe a hundred fifty in the town of Pigsend, and Allen couldn't be thinking they'd invite all of them to their wedding, surely.

Around eight, her three guests came down, helped themselves to a muffin, and continued their journeys to far-off places. Once they were out the door, Bev quickly stripped the dirty sheets off the beds and added fresh ones, tidying the rooms so they'd be ready for this evening's guests. She didn't expect a full house, but she found if she didn't have everything set, she'd end up regretting it later. The laundry, however, she set outside to tackle after her visit to Merv's.

With the inn ready for another night, and her bread working its magic, she headed down to the kitchen once more to retrieve her basket with the amulet pieces. She tucked three of Allen's muffins on top, wrapping them into the tea towel.

"Suppose there's no more delaying the inevitable," she said to Biscuit, who'd followed her into the kitchen. "Now, you stay here, boy. You know Merv won't let me in the door if you come with me."

Biscuit stared at her with his golden eyes, silently arguing with her.

"Well, because the last time you were there, you destroyed his house and tried to eat his yarn."

The laelaps sat on the floor and hung his head.

"Oh, here." Bev tossed one of the muffins to the ground, which was eaten in two bites. "There you go. I'll be back in a bit."

The weather was lovely, and the town of Pigsend was bustling under the bright blue sky. Ida and Vellora Witzel, the butchers who lived next door, waved at Bev as she passed their shop. Bev popped her head in to order dinner ("four pounds of chicken, please") before continuing. Earl Dollman, the carpenter, was in the town square building scaffolding for Ramone Comely's dragon fountain, a replacement for the one that had been a victim of the sinkhole fiasco a few months ago. Jade Medlem, the mason, was talking with Ramone's brother about the exact specifications for its base. Bev waved at the quartet as she walked by, grateful they were too engrossed in their conversations to ask what she had in her basket or why she was carrying her glowing stick in the middle of the day.

She kept a brisk pace as she left the center of town behind, walking by farmlands that were starting to green up with the arrival of spring. Trent

Scrawl was hunched over what Bev assumed would be more of his award-winning pumpkins, but were, as of now, small green vines. Bev didn't want to distract him, so she kept walking.

The entrance to Merv's tunnel was far out of town, made during the sinkhole debacle when Merv had come to the surface to find out who was causing the earthquakes. The shaking hadn't just destroyed buildings in Pigsend; Merv's house had been in danger of collapsing, too. Bev had taken a shine to the moleman, and the two had become friends in the following few months.

She found his tunnel nestled in the rolling hills beyond the farms and gingerly stepped down into the darkness. Her glowing stick, which she'd tucked under her arm, came to life, illuminating the path. It was quite rough, with bumps and other tripping hazards, but Bev managed to keep her footing all the way down.

Eventually, Merv's quaint house, with orange shutters and a green door, came into view. As Bev approached, the size of it became more apparent, with the doorknob at her shoulder and the welcome mat the size of Bev's kitchen table.

She rapped on the door, then took a step back and waited. After a moment, it swung open revealing a large creature nearly three heads taller than Bev, covered from head to toe in black fur with long claws and a pink snout. His whiskers twitched, and his dark eyes twinkled with excitement.

"Bev!" He opened the door wider. "Well, isn't this a lovely surprise. Come in, come in. I was just about to drink another cup of tea." He tilted his nose toward her. "Is that blueberry I smell?"

"Fresh from Allen's bakery," Bev said, lifting the basket as she passed.

"Oh, brilliant!"

He offered her a seat in his cozy little living room as he continued on into the kitchen to see to the tea. Nearly every surface of the room was covered in some kind of knitted decor. Next to the sizable chair, there was a basket of yarn and a half-finished scarf or blanket, Bev wasn't sure which. She settled onto the well-worn couch, looking around at what else was new.

"You've been busy?" she called into the kitchen.

"Oh, quite. You know me. I like to keep the claws moving."

He reappeared with a tea kettle that held several gallons of tea and two cups the size of Bev's bread-mixing bowl. Bev watched with a thin smile as he filled hers to the brim.

"Sugar?" he asked.

"No, thank you." She picked up the cup with effort and took a sip.

"So, dear Bev, to what do I owe the pleasure of your visit?" He picked up the half-finished knitting project and started working on it, his gaze on Bev.

"Another interesting curiosity happening in Pigsend?"

"Well, yes, but not Pigsend, per se," she said, revealing the amulet pieces. "Have you ever seen something like this before?"

He peered into the basket and frowned. "No, I can't say I have. What is it?"

"I believe they're connected to my past," she said, placing the basket on the table. "When I've handled them, I've had some visions. I think I was in the Battle of Eriwall..." She paused, looking at Merv. "Are you familiar?"

He shook his head. "With how bloody and horrific that war was, I try to keep my knowledge of it to a minimum."

"Well, I would, as well, except there's a soldier named Dag Flanigan who seems keen to discover who I was before Pigsend," Bev said. "Can't imagine why I'm so interesting to him, but he said he was 'looking into' my past. It's better to be prepared instead of being surprised, you know? But the only clue I have is this amulet. I was hoping you might be able to tell me something about it."

He picked up one piece and inspected it. "I'm no expert in talismans and amulets and things of that nature. But I do know someone who is."

Bev perked up. "Really? Who?"

"A dear friend lives over in Lower Pigsend—a scribe who keeps records of all things magical." He nodded. "And as it turns out, I was planning on walking down there today. Need to run some errands. I would be happy to take you there."

"Lower Pigsend." Bev nodded. She'd had a hunch if Merv didn't know the answer, he'd take her to the mysterious underground town. Merv had described it as a town of magical creatures, where something like a magical sheep with purple wool wouldn't be looked at twice. But exactly what else was in that town, she didn't know. "How far is it?"

"Not far. A few minutes' walk." He rose. "Shall we?"

Chapter Two

There were two doors in Merv's house, the one Bev always entered and another on the other side of the living room she could've sworn hadn't been there the first few times she'd visited. Out the second door, the tunnel was just as dark and difficult as the one Bev usually took. It was all she could do to keep her footing on the uneven terrain.

"So…has this city always been here?" Bev asked, hoping Merv might slow his quick gait if he was too busy talking.

"Of course! Well, not in its current state, of course. Before all the magical creatures moved in, it was something of a desolate place. Really only good for grumpy misanthropes and trolls and things like that. Then the queen decided there wasn't a place for magical creatures in the upper world, and they started trickling in. Before long, it was practically overflowing with everything from centaurs to fairies to imps and trolls!"

"And the queen still has no clue?" Bev frowned, thinking about all the magical hunters who'd been through Pigsend lately. "That seems unlikely."

"Right about the time the place was busting at the seams, a lovely wizard by the name of Percival Bloom showed up. He was able to cast all manner of spells to expand the cave from the cramped living quarters it had been and protect its inhabitants. This spell keeps everyone who's in, in. And everyone who's out, out."

Bev stopped. "Then why are we going? This spell should keep *me* out, right?"

"Well, yes. But…" He demurred, waving her to follow him. "When they cast this spell, it ran right through my house. For some reason, I'm able to come and go without much trouble. And clearly, since you were able to see the door to Lower Pigsend, you're exempt, too. Must be the placement of my home or some other oversight in the spell." He gestured to the tunnel. "Just be sure to keep that between us. The magistrate has some…er…*zealous* individuals keeping the peace. And I'd hate to get on their bad side."

Bev eyed him. "What if a queen's soldier found

your tunnel? The one going to your front—er, back door?"

He waved her off. "They would have to go through my house to get to Lower Pigsend. I'm quite sure I would notice."

Bev had some doubts about the security of that but left it alone. This was Merv's world, and she didn't know enough about magic to say otherwise. Besides, there were only a few people who knew Merv's tunnel existed, and it was a way from the main road, in a spot no one really walked, so she supposed it was all right.

"Ah, here we are!"

The tunnel's exit was up ahead, with a few houses visible just on the other side. Bev squinted as she stepped out into a large cave that stretched high overhead, but was impossibly crammed with buildings almost sitting on top of one another. And the *people!* If one could even call them people. There were humans to be sure, but also half-human, half-horse creatures, tall, pale men with pointed ears, even a man who seemed to be covered in scales with a fishlike head. A woman with a tall black hat waved gnarled sticks that transformed the pink flowers on her front porch to purple. And a creature with *three dog heads* walked by carrying a bag with potatoes sticking out of them.

"What in the..."

"Hurry up, Bev! We're headed this way."

Merv had gotten too far ahead, and Bev could scarcely believe he was the least odd thing on the street. She unstuck her feet from the ground and hurried over to meet him, unable to hide her gawking.

"Merv, this is… Goodness gracious, what a place!"

"Fascinating, isn't it? I'd guess it's the most concentrated collection of magical creatures in the country now," he said. "Everything that the queen doesn't like can be found in this town."

Of course, having no memory of the world before the war, Bev only knew Pigsend, with its normal people and problems. She'd come across a magical person here and there—Ida Witzel and Allen's late mother Fernley—but they could hide their abilities well enough. The man with large antlers who crossed their path would certainly be noticed on the streets of Pigsend. As would the family of rather large mice, led by the mother (as evidenced by the apron tied around her waist) who chittered at her children—at least twenty of them. Each of them carried a piece of yellow cheese.

"Amazing that all of these people can fit," Bev said as they walked past a giant, yellow chicken almost the size of Merv, who was sweeping the front step of a store marked *Apothecary*. She couldn't help but stare at him, trying to suss out the manner in which he could hold a broom with his feathered hand. Eventually, she realized she was being rude, and scampered after Merv.

"There's plenty of magic running through the walls around here," Merv said. "Even so, the wizard had to really roll up his sleeves and do some fancy spellcasting to make it all work. Most everything in town has been touched by Percival in some way, from the nails in the homes to the butter on the table."

"Butter?" Bev eyed a pair of tall, translucent-skinned creatures with pointed ears and long, silvery hair as they walked by, discussing a book one of them was holding. "How does one make butter from magic?"

"A replication spell. Percival can take a single piece of something and turn it into more," Merv said. "So you have one piece of cheese, then you have two. Two turns into four, and so on."

Bev turned to look at the world around. "So everyone's just eating food touched by magic?"

"Well, not *everything* is touched by magic," he said. "I know they've been able to grow root vegetables down here pretty well. And, of course, they've got the livestock who provide milk and eggs. But..." He paused. "Well, yes, everything else is touched by magic. But it hasn't caused any problems, and there's no need to go to the surface."

"I'm sure it's safer that way, too," Bev said, her gaze drawn to a pair of pointy-eared creatures with bright purple wings standing in front of a collection of small houses that barely came up to Bev's knee. "Is everyone here a refugee of the queen?"

He nodded. "Except me, of course. But the magistrate doesn't mind me coming or going."

"Magistrate," Bev repeated. "You mentioned them earlier. Who's that?"

"They're the law in town," he said. "Their offices are somewhere in the Merchant's House, and they have a pair of guards who like to cause trouble for anyone who's not toeing the line. Which is why I'd *prefer* if they didn't know about my tunnel."

"I see."

"Anyway, let's not dwell on that, shall we?" He picked up his speed. "There's a dear friend I'd like you to meet."

"The scribe?"

"Oh, we'll get to him soon enough. But this is someone else. I'm sure she's dying to meet you." He tapped his claws together excitedly.

"She…knows about me?" Bev frowned. "How would she know about me?"

"Well, I've told her, of course."

"Merv." Bev narrowed her gaze. "You told me you weren't telling people about your little…well, *secret*." She eyed a pair of fairies as they floated by, leaving a trail of glowing dust behind them. "Which would, presumably, include your friend who lives on the other end of that *secret*."

"Lillie wouldn't tell a soul. I'm her best customer, after all." He walked toward a store marked *Bakery* and opened the door. "Come in, come in!"

Inside, it smelled much like Allen's place—sweet, with hints of spices and cinnamon, but there was something else, too. Almost nutty. A large display case carried an array of intricately designed sweets: small hand pies with sugar-crusted toppings, yellow custards in delicate casings, a multi-layered cake with gooey white frosting. Behind the case, a woman with coiled, golden hair stood behind a long table, working dough. She was very pale, with rosy cheeks smattered with a few freckles, and her blue eyes lit up when she saw Merv.

"Well, aren't you a sight for sore eyes?" she said, her voice high and melodious as she dusted her hands on her apron. "My dear Merv." Her attention turned to Bev, and her eyes widened even more. "And who've you brought with you?"

"Bev, this is Lillie Dean. Lillie, this is Bev," he said, gesturing to her.

"Bev. Oh…Bev? *The* Bev?" Lillie gasped and looked at Merv. "Merv, you scoundrel. The magistrate will close your tunnel if they finds out you brought a topsider in here!"

"Who's going to tell him?" Merv asked with a look.

"Not me, for sure." Lillie stepped out from

behind the counter and shook Bev's hand. "It's wonderful to meet you. Merv's told me all about your exploits."

"I'm sure he's exaggerated. I'm just a simple innkeeper."

"An innkeeper who rescued the town from sinkholes, saved the Harvest Festival, solved a blackmail mystery, *and* managed to keep a notorious magic-hunter away from a young dragon shifter?" Lillie scoffed. "Sure, a *simple* innkeeper."

"Well, when you put it like that," Bev said, blushing as she inspected the sweets in the case more closely. Although Allen had been taking great pride in his work lately, next to these delicacies, his pies and muffins looked positively amateurish. "Lillie, you certainly have a talent. I've never seen such beautiful confections."

"Try one! I'm dying to know how they compare." She plucked a beautiful multi-layered cake from the case and placed it on the counter, pushing it toward Bev with a starry-eyed expression.

"Oh, I can't—"

"I *insist*," Lillie said with a grin.

"Well, if you say so."

Bev brought the cake to her nose and sniffed. She got hints of nuts, sugar, cinnamon, and something earthy. She took a hesitant bite, and the flavors that filled her mouth were more sweet and spicier than anything she'd ever had before. There was something else, too—something familiar and unexpected.

Bev inspected the cake, which had small flecks of orange in the sponge.

"Well?" Lillie bit her lip. "What do you think?"

"It's magnificent," Bev said, trying for some restraint as she took another bite instead of stuffing the entire thing into her mouth. "But is that... carrot?"

"Drat." Lillie deflated. "I was hoping it wouldn't be noticeable."

"Oh, don't get me wrong, it's the most delicious carrot I've ever had in my life," Bev said, pulling the paper off so she could take another bite. "I've just never had... Never even *thought* to..." She couldn't help herself and took the largest bite she could fit in her mouth. Who knew carrots could taste so outrageously divine?

"See? I told you they're delicious, Lillie," Merv said. "No need to trouble yourself with perfection when they're already perfect."

"I just feel like I can do better." The baker adjusted the sweets in the case. "Poor excuse for a pobyd I am."

Bev gasped. "Pardon, did you say you were a *pobyd?*"

"Yes." Lillie flashed a smile and gestured to the confections in her case. "Isn't it obvious?"

Bev hadn't ever met a full pobyd; Fernley

Mackey was merely descended from one, and had some use of the magic. But based on Lillie's artistry, Fernley was a shadow of the real thing.

"Did you know the Mackeys in Pigsend?" Bev asked.

"Mackeys?" She tapped her chin before shaking her head. "Doesn't ring a bell. But I lived in Sheepsburg before moving here. Why?"

"They're the bakers in Pigsend," Bev said. "My neighbors, actually. Fernley's passed on, but her son Allen is still there. We thought Fernley might've had some pobyd in her. But she never made anything as good as this."

"I do the best with what I have," Lillie said.

"What does that mean?" Bev asked, finishing the rest of it. She couldn't find a single reason for Lillie's devaluation of her talents.

"I don't suppose Merv's told you about some of the *limitations* that come with living here, has he?" Lillie asked. "Like our food?"

Bev shook her head. "He mentioned that Percival uses some kind of magic to make most of your diet, right?"

"Yes." Merv nodded. "Certain things do better when replicated by magic. Nuts are very hardy. You can make thousands of pounds of almonds or walnuts from a single handful. But more delicate foods like grains and fresh fruit disintegrate when one tries to make more of them with the replication spell."

Lillie sighed. "I remember making such beautiful things with fruit and wheat flour. Now all I have are nuts and carrots, and instead of fresh strawberries, I'm using beets to make jam. And all my baked goods are made with nut flour. I'm grateful there are cows and chickens bred down here to give me milk and eggs, at least."

"Yes, but…" Bev gestured to the case. "That was *incredible.* Flour or no, carrots or whatever else you used, I can't recall when I've had a better-tasting pastry."

"You're too kind." Lillie blushed. "You're welcome to come back any time and tell me how delicious my pastries are."

"That sounds like a horrible idea," Bev said. "I may never leave. And I've been spoiled by a baker who lives next door."

"But he's not full pobyd, right?" Lillie asked.

"As far as we know, neither was his mother, but she still had a bit of pobyd magic," Bev said. "That's most of the magic up there now. For example, my friend Ida is a butcher who can lift things three times her weight. But nobody thought that was out of the ordinary."

"It's been so long since I've been topside," Lillie said. "I'd ask you to smuggle me some flour or a jar of jam, but I'd hate to have the magistrate's men ransack my shop in search of it."

"Surely, they can't be that bad," Bev said. "After all, there's that spell keeping everyone safe, right? Why would they need to bother people inside the town?"

"Well, you're here, right?" Lillie shrugged. "Maybe they've got reasons they just aren't sharing with us."

"I think they just like bothering people," Merv said. "Don't want the townsfolk to believe they're not doing their jobs."

"Let's just hope they don't find out about that topside tunnel of yours, Merv," Lillie said. "After all, I'm not sure what I'd do if I lost my best customer."

"Speaking of…" His whiskers twitched. "Dare I ask if you have those cookies available?"

"You like the carrot-walnut, right?" Lillie asked, turning to look at the oven in the back. "I've got a batch of caramel-pecan baking right now, but as soon as they're out, I'll whip you up some of your favorites. Just pop in on your way back, and they're all yours."

"You're a saint, Lillie," Merv said. "Come, Bev. We must get on to visit the scribe and get you back to the inn."

"Oh, goodness, that's right." Bev glanced at the time. More had passed than she would've liked, but there was still plenty of day left for her to get back to the inn. "Lead the way."

Chapter Three

They left Lillie's bakery, and Merv seemed much more chipper at the promise of freshly baked cookies. Bev, too, with her stomach full of magic-laden carrot cake, was practically levitating. She couldn't help but think it was a *very* good thing there wasn't a full-blooded pobyd next door. She'd probably eat herself silly if Allen had nearly the same abilities.

"No wonder the queen put pobyds on her list of naughty creatures," Bev said. "With tempting pastries like that."

"Why do you think I'm so keen on visiting her?" His whiskers twitched. "They lose their potency after a few days, then they're just regularly delicious instead of indescribably so."

"I can't imagine," Bev said. "Lillie really doesn't need to worry about not having flour. She's certainly done well with what she has."

Merv nodded. "She's always experimenting. Last week, she knocked my socks off with a pecan pie."

"I bet that was incredible," Bev said. "But, Merv, if I can use your tunnel, and you can use your tunnel, why can't Lillie go to the surface? Or at the very least, couldn't I bring her something?"

"If you did, she'd run afoul of the magistrate," Merv said. "They might do something drastic, like kick her out. And despite her complaints, it really is the safest place for a pobyd to live. Otherwise, she'd be at the mercy of the queen's people."

A large, hulking creature who looked more like a pile of rocks than anything else, came lumbering by. "And depending on how one *looks*, too."

He chuckled. "You saw the stir I caused with my appearance, and I'm just an ordinary moleman."

"Merv, there's nothing about you that's ordinary," Bev said with a smile.

They continued through town, and Bev counted the different kinds of shops that lined the streets. A cobbler, a tavern, even an artist shop with paintings priced to sell. Below her eye level, more shops were squeezed between the buildings, clearly catering to the smaller clientele. One was a cheesemonger's shop, another was selling small potions to aid in the…was that the strengthening of fairy wings?

"Lillie said there were cows and chickens here," Bev said, wrenching her gaze away. "Where in the world are they kept? And if there's no grain to give them, what do they eat?"

"Oh, you have to remember that things work a little differently down here," Merv said. "A lot of the houses keep their animals in magically expanded rooms. The Merchant's House has rows and rows of pens for all manners of different creatures." He paused. "And as for what they eat, I believe it's usually potato scraps and things like that."

She tried to imagine Sin going without any grain and chuckled. "You know, I don't think you're the only one with a tunnel into Pigsend. Upper Pigsend, whatever you'd like to call it."

"No?"

"If you recall, Bathilda was going to be selling her tanddaes to someone from here," Bev said. "How did they get them here if everything is supposedly closed off?" She put her hands on her hips. "Don't suppose a herd walked through your front door, did they?"

He chuckled. "Don't tell me you've got another mystery on your mind."

"No, no." Bev smiled. "But it is curious, don't you think?"

"As with most things, I'm sure the spell cast on this place has its quirks and exceptions." He smiled.

"And speaking of, if you'd like to see where all that protection comes from, it's right up ahead."

He pointed to a large fountain that reminded Bev of the long-since-destroyed one in the Pigsend town square. But as they drew closer, magic brushed against her skin and in the back of her mind. In the center, right above the fountaining water, was a floating…well, it looked like a regular water pail, except that it was sparkling and rotating in the air.

"What is that?" Bev asked.

"The talisman where the spell comes from," Merv said. "It's quite an effort to cast a spell, and one that maintains its strength over several days, months, years? That takes even more. A talisman helps by serving as the conduit for all that magic and keeps itself going even after the wizard turns his attention to something else."

"But why is it a pail?" Bev asked, tilting her head to the side.

"Oh, you know, I'm not quite sure," Merv said. "I'm not an expert on magical spells or talismans, but I do know that a spell cast on an item can be enhanced by the purpose of that item, if that makes sense. A container spell on a container. Or so I imagine."

"Suppose that makes sense," Bev said. There certainly was a lot to know about magic, not that it mattered in Bev's day-to-day life. "Well, good to know they figured a way to make it last without taxing the poor fellow. He must be powerful to keep all this afloat."

"Indeed, he is." Merv beckoned her to follow. "Come, come. The scribe is up ahead."

They continued down another road, full of shops and houses, creatures big and small, until Bev spotted the one marked *Steward Bigfeather, Scribe and Archivist*. Bev assumed it was similar to the job of Max Sterling, the local librarian. He seemed the only one in town who kept a record of things, including the town almanac.

But Max, at least, kept some semblance of order in his library, whereas this place seemed a hodgepodge mess of books, scrolls, and loose papers. Every square inch of space was taken, with something crammed into every shelf, nook, and cranny in the room. One counter in the front was halfway empty, but it was flanked on either side by towers of books leaning precariously toward each other.

"Max would have a heart attack if he saw this," Bev said, reading the titles on the nearest shelf. None seemed to be in any kind of order, with tomes on potion-making, moon cycles, and magical history all lumped in together. The only thing they had in common was that all these books would've been confiscated by Her Majesty's soldiers.

"Steward? Are you here?" Merv called.

There was a loud crash somewhere in the back of

the store before a mop of brown hair bustled through the tops of the stacks. Then, with a chirp, a figure hopped onto the counter, perfectly fitting between the two towers of books.

He was... Well, he looked like a giant *bird*. Complete with claws, feathers, beak... He almost resembled a sparrow in coloring and shape, except he was twice the size of Biscuit. And clearly, he wasn't just a big bird, based on the scrolls tucked under his wing that he placed on the table.

"Merv!" The sparrow snapped its jaws together in happiness. "What a wonderful surprise! I haven't seen you around in months. Don't tell me you've read through your last stack of books. I'm running out of things to offer you."

"No, no. Still working through them," Merv said. "Bev, Steward was one of the last to come down before the doors to Lower Pigsend permanently closed, and he's amassed quite the collection of books and other items that were banned when the queen took over."

"Some escaped at the very last second," Steward said with an affirming nod.

Max would've been proud. "Very nice to meet you, Steward. I'm Bev."

"Bev, *the* Bev?" The sparrow's small eyes swept to her, and she gave a half-smile as she tried not to stare at the peculiar way his beaked mouth moved as he spoke. "The one from the upper world?"

Bev turned to the moleman, pursing her lips. "*Merv*."

"I only told my dearest friends," he said, bristling. "I doubt either of them are going to have much to do with the magistrate, eh? Steward has to contend with their requests often enough that I doubt he'd seek them out intentionally."

"Bloody annoying, they are. Nog and Bola, that's their names." Steward clapped his beak together in frustration. "Every time they come by asking for something for the magistrate, it takes ages to put the shop right again." Steward turned to Bev. "Well, Bev, just down for a social visit, or are you in need of some light reading material?"

Bev reached into the basket hanging from her arm and pulled out the two pieces of the amulet. "I was hoping you could tell me what this is."

"Oh, my." He tapped the pieces as she laid them on the table before him. "These have seen some action, haven't they? Where did you find them?"

"Well, one was buried in my garden," Bev said. "The other was in a thicket down the road. I don't know where they came from, but they gave me terrible visions when I put them together. I think it was...my past."

"Ah, yes. Merv told me you haven't a clue who you were before you came to town." Steward took the two pieces in his feathered hands and turned them over. "I can't say I've ever seen these markings before, but there's a lot of knowledge in these books. And goodness knows I haven't read them all yet."

Disappointment settled in Bev's chest. "So you don't know what it is? Could it be a talisman like the one in the fountain?"

"It's possible, but amulets like these usually have a different purpose." He turned one of the pieces over a few times. "You see this right here?" He pointed to a small semicircle Bev hadn't noticed before. "It looks like this was worn on something hung from the neck, like a chain. It was probably worn to enhance or remove some ability."

"Can you tell what?" Bev asked.

"Not off the top of my head, but I assure you, I've probably got the answers in the library." He turned to peer at the large stack behind him. "It may take me a while to find it, though. Would you mind very terribly leaving the pieces here with me so I might have a good reference?"

"Actually, I'd prefer it," Bev said, pushing the pieces over to the bird. "It seems like this town is much better suited to magical items that glow in the dark than Pigsend." She paused. "And if you don't happen to find out what it is, you're welcome to keep it or toss it. I'm not keen on getting it back."

"That eager to get rid of it?" Steward asked.

"The visions this amulet gives me are ones I'm not interested in revisiting," Bev said. "If they are my past, it's probably better off buried. But..." She eyed them. "It still would be nice to know what I'm dealing with. Just in case that past comes back in more than just visions."

Bev felt lighter leaving the amulet behind. At the very least, it was *out* of Pigsend, so if any more queen's soldiers came looking for it, Bev could honestly say it was gone.

Though thinking of the spate of soldiers who'd been through town reminded her of Claude, and how Bev had—unknowingly—almost led him to the front door of Lower Pigsend.

"Say, Merv," Bev said as they made their way toward Lillie's bakery. "You never saw Claude again, did you?"

"Hm?"

"The judge I brought to your house during the Harvest Festival," Bev said. "You remember him?"

"Claude? Yes, lovely fellow."

"Well, he turned out to be a queen's soldier, if you recall," Bev said. "Obviously, I hadn't a clue about Lower Pigsend, or about Claude's real identity. But do you think... Oh, Merv, I'd be devastated if he found out about this place."

"Rest assured, Percival's spell is working just fine," Merv said. "He wouldn't have been able to get five steps past my front door if not. Besides that, I never mentioned Lower Pigsend, so he wouldn't have known there was anything beyond my home."

"I suppose that's true," Bev said with a bit of relief. "I really should be more careful. Never know who might be hiding a secret identity."

They stopped by Lillie's bakery on their way out, and Bev couldn't help but sink her teeth into one of the freshly baked carrot-and-walnut cookies that Lillie had baked for Merv. They were smattered with what Lillie described as "magically replicated" chocolate chips. Bev couldn't taste the difference between what Allen had in his bakery and the delicious brown morsels melting on her tongue, and she was somewhat jealous that Merv had an entire dozen to take home.

"Take another, then," Merv said as they left the dim light of the town for the tunnel back to his house. "I insist. I can always get more from Lillie."

"Oh, all right. Maybe I'll bring it to Allen for inspiration." Bev plucked one of the still-warm cookies from the box. "If I can make it that long. It's quite tempting, all warm and melty as it is. That pobyd magic is something else. Can't believe I'm salivating over a vegetable."

"Maybe you could take some inspiration for yourself," Merv said. "I find cinnamon with carrot is quite the combination. You could try your hand at baking something other than rosemary bread. Perhaps something to test for the Harvest Festival. You are entering again, aren't you?"

"That's my plan," Bev said. "You know, I've

been tinkering with my process. Letting it sit for longer, using different amounts of ingredients. I hate to say the competition bug's got me, but I think it has. I'd very much like to win this year."

"I daresay you were robbed last year," Merv said.

"Well, the judge *did* indicate that she gave the first-place ribbon to someone else because she didn't want any claims of impropriety," Bev said. "So if we can avoid any mishaps this year, perhaps I'll prevail after all. But in the meantime, it is rather fun to see the differences between the two batches."

"If you need someone to give you an *expert* opinion, I'm more than happy to offer my services as an official taste-tester."

"You and Etheldra," Bev said. "But goodness, between those cookies and the muffins I brought you this morning, you should be set for a few days, at least."

He let out a contented sigh. "It's a good life I lead."

"And you're sure there won't be any problem with you bringing me to Lower Pigsend, or your friends knowing about me?" Bev said. "Those magistrate characters sound like they aren't very much fun to deal with."

"I wouldn't worry about me, Bev. I'm just a simple moleman who knits and eats baked goods. What sort of trouble can I cause?"

Chapter Four

It was nearly noon when Bev returned to
Pigsend. Or Upper Pigsend. It really was quite
confusing that both towns had the same name. Not
that she planned to discuss what she'd seen today
with anyone, except *maybe* Allen or Ida, who both
already knew about Merv's tunnel.

Biscuit was waiting for her, asleep by the
dormant fireplace, but he sprang to life as soon as
the door opened.

"Nobody came by?" Bev asked.

He let out a low ruff as he followed her into the
kitchen.

"Well, bit early for that, you know," Bev
muttered. "Hopefully, we'll get someone this

evening."

She placed the still-warm cookie from Lillie on the table and checked on her two rosemary bread doughs in their bowls. She poked the tops of them, comparing their texture, before replacing the towel. They weren't quite ready to shape yet but would be soon.

"Don't you dare."

Biscuit's nose was almost invisible as it inched closer to the cookie. One swipe of his tongue, and it would be on the ground. But as usual, he listened to Bev's warning tone and sat.

"Next time I visit Lower Pigsend, I'll be sure to bring you a magical cookie," Bev said. "Probably not a good idea for you to visit. You'd go crazy with all the magic." She paused, giving him a scrutinizing look. "You didn't come from Lower Pigsend, did you?"

She still hadn't a clue why he'd chosen her to be his meal ticket, as he'd just shown up in her compost pile during the Harvest Festival. She hadn't given it much thought since those early days, thinking maybe he'd accompanied someone from out of town and decided he liked it better at the Weary Dragon. But knowing there was an entire town of magical creatures down below gave her a new perspective on things.

"Well, I suppose it doesn't matter," Bev said. "You're here now. And we have laundry to do."

Arguably, it was Bev's least favorite chore, made only slightly more palatable now that the temperature outside was warm, and the sun dried the sheets quickly. She pulled her large, heavy bucket to the water pump and filled it, adding a bit of soap before starting on the pile of used sheets. Biscuit came out to lie in the sun, stretching his tiny body long and falling into a deep, relaxed sleep.

"Glad someone's getting a rest," Bev said, eyeing him. "Don't want to wait in the front room for any potential guests?"

He let out a loud snore.

"Fine."

As she worked, she thought about how one might do the laundry in Lower Pigsend. Soap, she assumed, might be magically replicated. Water might come from the ground itself. But how long would it take for sheets to dry when there wasn't a sun to work on them?

"Well, perhaps the wizard can just dry them magically," Bev said to a sleeping Biscuit.

The laundry took most of the afternoon, and when all the sheets were hanging on the line, it was time to shape her bread loaves for their second proof and start preparing the rest of dinner. The Witzels had dropped off the chickens, and Bev needed to rustle up some root vegetables to accompany them. As she headed for her root cellar (bringing along Biscuit, because she didn't quite trust him alone with that magical cookie), she thought about incorporating some of Lillie's unique combinations of spices with the side dishes. Cinnamon and carrot had never even crossed her mind before, but she had a hankering to experiment with that delicious combination herself.

"Of course, the taste could've been because Lillie's a pobyd," Bev said to Biscuit, as they walked back to the kitchen.

She scrubbed and skinned the potatoes and carrots, rough chopping them before adding them to the pan with the chickens. The cookie was still on the table, somehow still warm (*more of that magic?*) and the smell was enough to drive even *her* wild.

"I suppose we should get that cookie where it needs to go before one of us loses our nerve," Bev said, tossing the last of the carrots into the pan. "We've got a few hours before this needs to go into the oven anyway. Let's pay Allen a visit."

Inside his bakery, Allen was carefully icing a set of cookies, his face screwed up in concentration. But as soon as Bev walked in the door, he lowered the pastry bag and gave her a brighter grin than he'd worn earlier that day.

"Bev!" He dusted his hands on his apron. "To what do I owe the pleasure?"

"Brought you a little pick-me-up," Bev said, placing the cookie on the counter.

"What's that?" Allen asked. "Don't tell me

you're getting into sweets baking."

"Not me." Bev glanced around, making sure no one else was in the shop. "I went to visit Merv today, and he took me to a place called Lower Pigsend. Have you heard of it?"

He shook his head.

"Apparently, it used to be a very small place for gnomes and trolls, but once the queen got going, it became a haven for all manner of supernatural creatures," Bev said. "And there happened to be a pobyd by the name of Lillie who makes the most divine creations."

"A pobyd!" His eyes lit up with surprise. "Really? What's she like?"

"Pretty normal, in my view. But she was making the most incredible confections," Bev said. "Apparently, she can't get wheat to make flour down there, so she's had to make do with using ground-up nuts instead."

"No flour?" He blinked. "Why not?"

"Something to do with the magic down there," Bev said, not wanting to go into too much detail. "But Lillie doesn't seem to let it bother her. This cookie is made from ground up walnuts, some chocolate she said was made by magic, and—if you can believe it—*carrots*."

"Carrots? In a cookie?" He chuckled, leaning in to smell it. "That's the silliest… Oh. Oh, goodness." He took another whiff. "That smells absolutely delightful. And..." He poked it. "Wow, did you just bake it?"

"No, I think her magic keeps it warm. Merv said that the cookies he buys are delicious for days afterward."

"What I wouldn't give for *that* kind of magic," Allen said, rubbing his fingers together after touching it again. "And it does have magic. It sits on your skin." Another sniff. "I can't believe how amazing it smells."

"Give it a try," Bev said.

Allen broke off a small piece and popped it into his mouth. The realization of flavor took its time washing over his face, from surprise to curiosity to enjoyment to adoration. He licked his lips, speechless as he looked closer at the confection.

"Oh, my."

"Right?" Bev had to resist the urge to break off another piece for herself. "Who knew nuts and carrots could taste so divine?"

"It's like..." He took another bite. "Man, it's like my mom's cooking. But much more...*more*." He broke off another piece. "This is something else. I'd never be able to replicate this. And I certainly can't make nuts and carrots meld together like this."

"Well, I thought you might be inspired by it," Bev said. "Perhaps something to experiment with for the winter months when the fruit fillings get a bit lean."

He broke the cookie apart in his fingertips as he inspected it. "How in the world did she get these carrots chopped so finely? This is fascinating."

"If I go back, I'll be sure to ask," she said.

"Maybe you shouldn't. I can't be distracted by new things." He nodded to the front of his shop, where the half-iced cookies sat. "I'm just lucky there are a slew of birthdays coming up. Cakes fetch a good price, especially if I get them iced nicely enough, and they don't take too much time." He sighed. "Vicky stopped by this morning to provide me with her specifications for *our* cake."

Bev's eyes widened. "Baking your own wedding cake! Allen, really."

"Well, who else would do it?" Allen asked with a shrug.

Briefly, Bev thought of Lillie, and giving her the chance to bake with flour for something that wouldn't stay in Lower Pigsend. But that was probably just inviting trouble.

"I suppose you're right," she said after a moment. "But don't overextend yourself. I don't know what I'd do without my favorite baker."

"Are you sure I'm still your favorite?" He nodded to the crumbs on the counter. "I don't know if *I'm* still my favorite baker anymore."

"Allen, you'll always be number one in my heart," Bev said with a small laugh. There was movement outside the Weary Dragon Inn.

"Goodness, that's my cue. Looks like I've got the first guest of the night."

"Good luck," Allen said, sweeping the rest of the crumbs into his hand and tossing them into his mouth. "And if you happen to find another one of those cookies, don't be shy about bringing it over here."

~

"Hello there," Bev said, walking into the front room of the Weary Dragon. The man she'd seen was standing by the front desk and turned to beam at her.

"Hello! Are you the proprietor of this lovely establishment?" he asked, adjusting his small suitcase in his hand.

"I am," she said. "Name's Bev. Welcome to the Weary Dragon. Is this your first time in Pigsend?"

"It is," he said, as she walked around the front counter. "My name is Edward Murfin."

"Very nice to meet you," she said, sitting on her stool. "It's one gold coin per night, which includes your fill of dinner and one room to yourself with two beds."

"It'll just be me," he said, placing the coin on the counter. "Quite a lovely place you have here."

"What business brings you to Pigsend?" Bev asked, scribbling his name down on the guest log before handing him a key.

"Oh, this and that." He shifted the suitcase

again. "Just in town for the night before continuing on."

"We've had plenty of that lately," Bev said. "You'll be in room one."

"Much obliged."

~

Dinner was served at exactly six on the dot. The usuals—Etheldra Daws, Earl Dollman, and Bardoff Boyd, the schoolteacher—showed up on time, and the only new guest was the kind Mr. Murfin, who was more than complimentary about the meal, especially the bread.

"Well, if this is the meal, I daresay I may stay for more than a night!" Murfin said, heaping three pieces of bread onto his plate.

"Make sure to leave some for the rest of us." Etheldra Daws owned the tea shop in town and was one of Bev's most loyal—if blunt—customers.

"There's plenty for everyone," Earl said, queuing up behind her. "What changes did you make to the bread this morning, Bev?"

"Well, this is the usual loaf," Bev said, pointing to one basket. "And this one, I let sit for a minute before I started working the dough. I feel like it's a bit more even in the crumb, you know? But I leave it to my taste-testers to let me know what you think."

"Where were you headed this morning?" Earl asked as he helped himself to a piece from both loaves. "Another adventure to contend with?"

She chuckled. "Hardly. Just a social visit." Bev didn't feel comfortable talking about Lower Pigsend with the assembled crowd, especially with an unknown person like Mr. Murfin. One never knew who was a queen's soldier in disguise.

The last to join the group was Max Sterling, which reminded Bev of Steward and his large bookshop. The old librarian chatted with Bev for a minute, then took his plate to the table to join the rest as they were learning more about Mr. Murfin and why he was in town. After a pint of Bev's ale, he seemed a bit more willing to talk about his business, which usually happened with reticent guests at the Weary Dragon.

"Just for the night. Passing through on my way to Sheepsburg," he said with a pat on his stomach. "I'm a traveling salesman, so if anyone is in need of tinctures and medicines, I've got plenty to sell."

"We have an adequate apothecary in town, thank you very much," Etheldra said, her nose lifting upward.

Murfin started, but the two men seated at the table with him just shook their heads. Etheldra's bluntness was well-known, but it was always jarring to those who were passing through.

The rest of the dinner passed uneventfully, with the conversation pleasant and Etheldra's sharp tongue mostly held. Bev was lost in thought, thinking about what the denizens of Lower Pigsend might be eating for supper. Her carrots were bland and tasteless compared to the memory of those walnut-carrot cookies—not that Bev had done much more than cook them with the chicken.

"Etheldra," Bev asked, looking up as soon as the conversation lulled. "Would you be terribly offended if I used cinnamon in a dinner recipe one of these days?"

"Cinnamon? In dinner?" She made a face. "However did you think of that nonsense?"

She shrugged. "Well?"

"I think you need to quit tinkering with what you know is working just fine for you," Etheldra said, before muttering to herself. "Cinnamon in dinner. What's next? Chocolate for breakfast? Of all the things…"

Well, that was Bev's answer. If she was going to experiment with anything other than the bread, she'd have to make sure Etheldra's staples were always part of the menu.

One by one, the diners finished their meals and said goodbye, ending with Mr. Murfin, who once again asked Bev if she was in need of a tincture.

"Perhaps for sleep? Or sore feet?" he asked.

"Thank you, but I think I'll be just fine," Bev said. "If you require anything else this evening, please let me know."

Mr. Murfin walked up the stairs, and Bev set to

her evening chores, scrubbing the dishes and letting the large pan soak for a bit before she tackled it again. She eyed the leftover dough she'd use in the morning to make her three loaves of rosemary bread and put her hand on her hip as Biscuit sniffed the floor, licking up any crumbs she might've dropped in her cleaning.

"What do you think, B?" she asked. "Shall we try an overnight proof? See what happens?"

Biscuit wagged his tail, which was as good an answer as Bev was going to get from her laelaps. She assembled all her ingredients—flour, the leftover dough, barm, salt, and rosemary—and had just put them together when Biscuit lifted his head, his snout pointed at the door, and he barked softly.

"What is it?" Bev asked. "Is someone out there, Biscuit?"

He let out a low ruff and pushed the kitchen door open with his nose. Bev wiped her hands on her apron before removing it and following him out into the main room. Mr. Murfin wasn't there, and neither was anyone else.

"Biscuit, I don't—"

There was a knock at the front door.

"Odd." Bev glanced at the time. It wasn't wholly unheard of to get a guest at this hour, but it wasn't common.

She approached the door slowly and Biscuit let out a low growl.

"What is it?" Bev asked, pausing.

Another knock, this one more urgent.

Bev crossed the room and opened the door, but nothing could've prepared her for the sight before her, or the words that came out of the green-skinned, lumpy-headed guard's mouth.

"Bev of the Weary Dragon Inn. You're under arrest for the theft of the Lower Pigsend protective talisman."

Chapter Five

Bev stared at the two creatures, quite sure she was dreaming. The one who'd spoken *was* quite green and lumpy, with a gnarled face and two large canine teeth that jutted up from his lower jaw to beyond his top lips. He glared at her with his menacing golden eyes and rested his knobby hand on a club that looked made from rock. Next to him was a creature wearing the same dark brown uniform, but he had purple eyes, brown skin, and yellow spots smattered across his forehead.

"I'm sorry, what did you say?" she finally managed.

"You are under arrest for the theft of the Lower Pigsend talisman," the green one said, walking inside.

"That's absolute poppycock," Bev said. "And who are you anyway?"

"I'm Officer Nog, and this is Officer Bola of the Lower Pigsend Magistrate's office," he said. "And as I said, you are *under arrest* for the theft of—"

"I did no such thing," Bev said, putting her hand on her hip. "And how in the world are you here, anyway? I thought no one could get out of Lower Pigsend?"

"The magistrate made a special arrangement for us to hunt you down and retrieve what's been stolen," Bola said, stepping toward her.

Beside her, Biscuit growled, the hair on his back rising, and Bola retreated.

"Why do you think *I* took it?" Bev said.

"It's no coincidence that an outsider showed up in Lower Pigsend the same day it was stolen," Nog said. "You and that criminal moleman, Merv."

"Merv? Criminal?" She laughed. "You really must be without suspects."

Bola's eyes narrowed. "The moleman illegally created a tunnel to the upper world, then left it completely unguarded so anyone could just waltz into our world and take what didn't belong to them."

"It's not *completely* unguarded," Bev said. "Anyone who passes through would have to go through his home. And he said he hasn't seen a person come or go."

"And when he's not there?" Nog asked, quirking his very bushy eyebrow.

Bev had to admit they *might've* had a point there. "That's what the talisman is for."

"*Was* for," Bola replied.

Bev put her hand on her hip, concerned. Now that it was gone, there wasn't anything protecting Lower Pigsend from the queen's people. She could certainly understand why these two *lovely* individuals were keen to find it.

"Well, in any case, you're welcome to search the inn," Bev said, gesturing around her. "You won't find it here, though. I didn't take it, and neither did Merv." She paused as they hobbled toward the stairs. They'd be quite a sight for anyone who wasn't aware of Lower Pigsend's existence. "But you may want to leave room one alone. I've got a guest there who might be a bit…taken aback by your presence."

"Harrumph." Nog pulled out a small vial from his pocket. "Don't think we haven't thought of that."

He put a drop on his and Bola's heads, and before Bev's eyes, they transformed into normal-looking humans, though they somewhat kept their existing features. Bola's straw hair stayed the same, and Nog retained his height and bushy brows. And to boot, they were wearing a uniform not unlike the one the Pigsend sheriff wore.

"Well, by all means," Bev said, gesturing toward the stairwell. "You seem to have thought of everything."

They marched up the stairs, and Bev waited at the bottom, listening for the sounds of disbelief or anger from Mr. Murfin. But the gentleman was happy to allow the two guards entry, and before long, they came down the stairs, empty-handed.

"Take it that you didn't find what you were looking for?" Bev said.

"Not to our eyes, but we have better ways of searching," Nog said, pulling something round and shiny from his pocket.

Biscuit's nose perked up, but Bev gave him a look and he sat, his golden eyes not leaving the two guards.

Nog put the disc on the floor and stood back. It spun, levitating off the ground and glowing as it picked up speed. Then, just as quickly as it started, it slowed down before dropping dormant to the ground.

"Hmph."

"W-what does that mean?" Bev asked, sharing a confused look with Biscuit.

"It means you've clearly hidden the talisman somewhere else," he said.

"Oh, rubbish," Bev scoffed. "What in the world would I need with a talisman?"

"You dropped off a powerful, broken amulet

with Steward Bigfeather earlier today," Bola said. "Clearly, you were in need of another one."

"And if you talk with Steward, he'll tell you I haven't a clue what that amulet does," Bev said. "In fact, I told him to keep it. I don't want a thing to do with talismans or amulets. Not with all the queen's soldiers who show up in town without warning." She shook her head. "I haven't a use for magical things."

Nog pointed to Biscuit. "What about him? He's a laelaps."

"He stays for the food," Bev said.

The laelaps wilted.

"Oh, come now, Biscuit, you know I'm right," Bev said, before softening. "But I do enjoy your company as long as you aren't sneaking meat off the table."

He brightened and wagged his tail.

"Enough of this." Bola waved his arms. "We have one week of magic left, and—"

"What do you mean a week?" Bev asked. "So the town is still protected?"

"Yes, but unless we find that talisman, the magic will fade entirely, and a few thousand people will be in danger of being discovered," Nog said. "So if you don't produce the talisman right now—"

"What? You'll arrest me?" Bev folded her arms across her chest. "Look, why can't you just cast another spell? I've got a pail in the back. You're welcome to it."

They shared a look, and as they did so, the spell transforming them into regular-looking guards started to fade.

"It doesn't *work* like that," Nog said with an eye roll.

"We wouldn't expect a *human* like you to understand."

"Well, then..." Bev hated to even suggest it. "Can you just...close Merv's tunnel? If there's no way to reach the surface—"

"That won't matter to the queen's people," Bola said. "She has creatures who are familiar with the ground."

Gnomes. Bev knew all about them. While they seemed...nice enough, they did take their marching orders from the queen.

"You know, Merv's not the only one who's been traveling between Pigsends," Bev said, slowly. "There's another man—someone who was selling tanddaes. He was up on this side talking with one of the farmers. I overheard them a few weeks ago. Perhaps you should be harassing him."

Nog scoffed. "A likely story."

"Where is this mystery man?"

"I'm not sure, but I could find out," Bev said. "I'll go ask Bathilda tomorrow. I'm sure we can clear all this up."

They shared a look, and seemingly a silent

conversation, before turning back to Bev. "All right, *topsider*. If, as you say, you can find us the name of this person who *might* be in the business of dealing in tanddaes, we'll leave you be."

"And Merv?" Bev asked.

"Merv must still answer for his crimes," Nog said. "The townsfolk need to know that their magistrate is taking steps to prevent this sort of dangerous occurrence from happening again."

Bev clicked her tongue. "So you need a scapegoat."

"We didn't say that! He's guilty—"

"I'll give you that he was a bit reckless in creating the tunnel, and even more reckless for keeping it open," Bev said. "But he couldn't have known someone was going to steal the talisman, and he's not the one at fault here." She lifted her chin. "One *could* say that the magistrate's men are to blame for not guarding the talisman better."

"Now, wait a minute—"

"If I get you a name, Merv's off the hook," Bev said. "And I won't tell the good citizens of Lower Pigsend my theory of who's really to blame."

Another shared look. "Fine. Get us a name tomorrow, and you *and* Merv won't hear from us again."

That night, Bev couldn't sleep, and so she was up very early making her bread and speeding through her morning chores. She believed that if the talisman wasn't found, Nog and Bola would be back to throw her in…jail, she supposed? She hadn't seen one on her visit, but she'd only seen a fraction of the underground town.

Merv might not hate the idea of spending his days in a cell, just as long as there was ample tea and yarn for him to knit. But Bev couldn't abandon the Weary Dragon like that, nor could she let Merv be accused of leaving the door open when clearly others could come and go as they pleased.

"We'll get it all cleared up," she said to Biscuit as she worked her rosemary dough.

She'd checked on her overnight experiment and found it only moderately risen—exactly as she'd hoped it would be. So in case the rise was too slow, she made another batch of dough for this evening.

"We're going to go to Bathilda's first," Bev said, talking more to herself than to Biscuit. "Then we're going to ask around to see if anyone else has seen anyone funny. There's nobody new in town—"

Biscuit barked and seemed to point his snout up toward Mr. Murfin in room one.

"Other than him, yes." Bev squinted at the laelaps. "But he's such a dear. He couldn't possibly have stolen it. And the guards searched the inn."

The laelaps just stared at her.

"Unless, of course, he stashed it somewhere in town," Bev said, after a moment. "But how would he even know… Oh, bother. I'm talking to myself again."

Biscuit walked toward the kitchen door and scratched at it.

"Absolutely not," Bev said. "We don't search guests and their rooms."

He sat and whined.

"I'll let you sniff at him when he comes down." She tapped her finger against her chin. "Maybe we ask him to stay for breakfast. That should give you enough time to really search him, eh?"

Biscuit let out a ruff, and Bev took that as a yes.

"You stay here and keep a nose out for him," Bev said. "I'm headed next door for a pastry."

Ruff.

"Yes, I'll get you something, too."

In the dim, early morning light, she walked over to Allen's bakery and found him already up and at work on the delicacies of the day. There were a few carrot scraps on the counter, and Bev could only imagine what Allen might be doing to replicate Lillie's recipe. But she didn't have time for that today.

"Oh, Bev!" he said as she walked in the door. "You're out early. Did you have a guest?"

"I do," Bev said, before pausing. "You didn't… You didn't happen to go to Merv's yesterday after we talked, did you?"

"Can't say that I did," he said. "Why?"

Bev told him briefly about the missing talismans and the two guards who'd visited her the night before, and the baker's brows lifted higher and higher as the story went on.

"I can only assume they didn't find it, because if they had, they would've been knocking down my door again," Bev said. "I'm going to Bathilda's today, but I wanted to have Biscuit sniff out my guest from last night."

"Because they usually end up staying in your inn, right?" Allen said with a chuckle. "Here. I've just made a batch of muffins for Etheldra. You're welcome to as many as you like."

Bev grabbed three—two for Mr. Murfin and one for Biscuit—paid Allen then headed back to the Inn. She left two on the counter, giving Biscuit half of one and eating the other half herself then propped the door open. The minutes passed by with excruciating slowness, and Bev had to remind herself that her guest was probably *not* as keen to get up and get going as she was.

Finally, well past eight in the morning, Mr. Murfin appeared at the top of the stairs, wearing his traveling clothes and carrying his bag. He looked refreshed and happy, but people could put on all kinds of airs.

"Good morning," Bev said, giving Biscuit a meaningful glance. "Did you sleep well?"

"I slept incredibly! What was that amazing fabric

of the knitted blanket?"

"Oh, um." Biscuit had walked over to Murfin but hadn't quite gotten close enough to sniff. "I'm not quite sure. My dear friend Merv made it for me." She tilted her head. "He's from nearby. Perhaps you've seen his house?"

Murfin glanced at Biscuit, whose nose was twitching as it inspected his bag. "Is your dog… erm…well?"

"Very well." He seemed interested in *something*, but it was hard to tell if it was magic or just a nice block of cheese. "Have a muffin. On the house. The baker dropped them off a few hours ago hoping to get some opinions."

"Oh, no, thank you." He patted his stomach. "If I have something sweet so early, it sets me in a mood for the rest of the day."

Bev should've asked for Allen's famous breakfast biscuits. "Well, then how about a cup of tea before you get on your way?"

He hesitated, but relented. "A tea sounds lovely. But after that, I really must be leaving."

"Brilliant. I'll get the kettle on."

Bev worked quickly, putting the kettle on the fire in the front room instead of the kitchen, and trying to engage her guest in conversation to keep him from looking like he was ready to bolt. He seemed more uncomfortable than the day before, sitting on the edge of the seat, his eyes darting to the door.

"Did you sleep well?" Bev asked.

"I believe you already asked that, innkeeper," he replied lightly.

"So I did." Bev stoked the fire, keeping a wary eye on Biscuit as he skulked around behind Murfin's chair. "I'd think you were quite the traveler, selling tinctures and the like. Do you usually stay local to… where was it, Sheepsburg?"

He nodded, twisting his hands together. "Business demands travel from time to time."

"I suppose if one needs more exotic ingredients," Bev said. Biscuit's nose was getting awfully close to the—

The laelaps pounced, jumping on the suitcase and pawing at the locks.

"Biscuit, down!" Bev cried, popping to her feet and running over as Murfin cried out in surprise.

"What is he doing?" Murfin said, swatting him away.

But the laelaps was nothing if not stubborn, and before either of them could pull him off, the suitcase sprang open, and the contents fell out—a few pairs of spare pants, some socks, and one very large vial of sparkling purple potion.

"I'm so sorry," Bev said, pulling him off. "I haven't a clue what's gotten into him. Maybe he was attracted to whatever's in that vial."

"Why would a dog care what's in my suitcase?"

Murfin asked, his face bright red as he gathered his things quickly. He caught Bev's gaze as he put his hand around the purple potion and licked his lips. "It's…um…a tincture for anti-aging."

"Is it now?" Bev couldn't help but notice the distinct lack of other vials in his bag. In fact, there looked to be just the one. How he was planning to fulfill anyone who took him up on his many offers, Bev didn't know.

"I…should probably be going."

He was out the door before Bev could say another word.

"Well, that went…awful," Bev said to Biscuit, who still had one of Mr. Murfin's socks in his mouth. "But at least he didn't take the talisman?"

Biscuit spat the sock out and sniffed the floor where the suitcase had been. Definitely magical but probably unrelated to the happenings in Lower Pigsend.

"Well, I suppose we've got to pay Bathilda a visit, eh?" Bev said with a sigh as she stood. "Hopefully, it won't be as disastrous as Mr. Murfin."

Based on Biscuit's low ruff, he was about as confident as she was.

Chapter Six

Bathilda lived on the west side of town, and while historically, she and Bev had gotten along fine, the last few times Bev had gone to see her were under mysterious, and somewhat strained, circumstances. After Alice Estrich's barn had been destroyed, Biscuit had gone sniffing in her neighbor Bathilda's yard and nearly ended up on the wrong end of an arrow. Bathilda had insisted neither Bev nor her laelaps set foot on her property again, which had, of course, piqued Bev's curiosity.

Under the cover of darkness, Bev had snuck back onto Bathilda's land to see if she might be the cause of all the property destruction. Instead, Bev found a herd of purple sheep-like creatures called tanddaes and overheard a conversation between Bathilda and a mystery man about selling them to Lower Pigsend. When Bev had later confronted her about the sheep, Bathilda hadn't given any indication of who she was selling to or where the sheep were going, just that they'd be gone soon.

How, exactly, Bev was going to broach the subject today was beyond her, but she'd come up with something.

The sun was warm and the temperature pleasant as Bev walked the narrow road out of Pigsend. The Weary Dragon Inn sat on the edge of town, and if one kept traveling west, they'd be met by rolling hills of farmland. Out this way, most of the farmers grew produce, and already there were long rows of green. The farmers' market was due to start any day now, and Bev was looking forward to eating something other than meat and root vegetables.

Bathilda lived about fifteen minutes from town, in a nice little home with a thatched roof and wooden walls painted white. The front porch was disarmingly welcoming, and Bev held her breath as she walked up the stairs. It was anyone's guess how Bathilda might react to her presence—and Bev had a feeling it would have a lot to do with whether the farmer had managed to sell her magical sheep or not.

Knock, knock, knock. "Bathilda? It's Bev."

She took a step back and waited.

After a few minutes, she rapped again, calling, "Bathilda? Are you home?"

Again, she waited, but there wasn't an answer.

"Hm."

Bev craned her neck to peer inside the house, but the curtains were drawn. With her hands in her pockets, she walked around the house, calling for Bathilda as she went. She passed empty fields where Bathilda should've been growing her gourds, potatoes, and carrots, around to the barren fields where she'd once seen strawberries. No sign of her.

Bev held her breath and walked toward the thicket of trees that had once held the tanddaes. The fence that Earl had constructed for her was still there, and when she inspected it closely, Bev found purple wool snagged in the timber, but no sheep. And yet again, no Bathilda either.

"Huh."

Bev turned on her heel and walked the length of the property again, hopping the fence in-between. Alice, at least, had been much friendlier to Bev in recent weeks, and her fields were already bearing some early spring berries. Alice's barn had been the unfortunate casualty in PJ's haphazard transformations, but it had been rebuilt perfectly by the trio of old ladies that Bev had affectionately called the grannies.

Alice was inside her barn, feeding her horse some hay and oats. She brightened when she saw

Bev. "Well, howdy, Bev. What brings you out this way? Farmers' market isn't getting started for another few days."

"Oh, is it that time already?" Bev asked with a smile. "Glad to hear it."

"Early days still. Lots of baby vegetables, but my berries have come in nicely already. Going to be a banner year, I believe."

"That's wonderful," Bev said. "I actually was looking for Bathilda. Have you seen her?"

Alice shook her head. "Not for a month, at least. She told me she was headed south for a spell. Seemed to have decided to take a holiday."

Bev's hopes sank. "Gone? Did she say when she'd be back?"

"She didn't. But I can't expect her to be gone too much longer, else she'll miss the planting season." Alice frowned, seeming to read Bev's expression. "What's the matter? Don't tell me more houses have gone down in town?"

"No, nothing like that," Bev said, forcing a smile. "Thanks. If you happen to see her, can you tell her to come by?"

"I will."

Bev turned to leave but stopped. "You didn't… see any kind of queen's soldier at her property, did you?"

"No, can't say that I did," Alice said. "Haven't seen one of those around in some time. Why? You don't think Bathilda's got anything over there that would interest Her Majesty, do you?"

"Of course not." Bev forced another smile. "Have a good one, Alice."

~

The walk back into town was slow as Bev pondered her next move. She'd promised Nog and Bola she'd give them a name in exchange for them leaving her and Merv alone, and her one lead was inconveniently out of town. She'd have to think of something else.

It was possible someone else in town was hiding a similar secretive herd of magical creatures, but that would take time Bev didn't have. Venturing down into Lower Pigsend and looking for the mystery man there was another option, but she hadn't seen his face, and from the brief time she'd spent there, the town was much more populated than Pigsend.

Biscuit was waiting for her in the inn, and she knelt to pat him on the head. "You don't have any other ideas, do you?"

He plopped his butt on the ground and tilted his head toward her.

"You're always so helpful." Bev rose. "Suppose I should get to work on dinner, eh? Etheldra won't care if I've been arrested, only that there's no stew on."

Bev worked with her mind elsewhere, nearly taking off the tip of her finger with her knife while cutting potatoes. She decided to take a break and visit the Witzels for a chat and a good distraction from the problems on her mind.

"Hi, Bev!" Ida said as she walked inside. "How was your trip to visit Merv?"

So much for the distraction. "Oh, well…"

"That good, huh?" Ida put down her knife. "What's going on?"

Bev told her about what had transpired down in Lower Pigsend, earning a look of surprise from the butcher, especially as Bev told her about being visited by the two officers of the magistrate.

"Goodness."

"I'm worried about Merv. They're just going to arrest him with no proof if I don't find out who really stole it," she said with a look. "Or worse, arrest *me*."

Ida tutted. "Didn't I see someone staying at the inn? Maybe they stole it."

"Left early this morning—in a hurry, I might add, after Biscuit almost tore his bag to shreds," Bev said. "He was carrying some kind of magical potion, but I doubt it had anything to do with the missing talisman."

She leaned on the counter. "Anyone else?"

"The only lead I had was Bathilda," Bev said. "She had some…items she was hoping to sell in Lower Pigsend. I overheard her talking about it with someone."

"Were you *sneaking* again?" Ida chuckled.

"Only because she'd threatened me with a crossbow," Bev said. "And this was a few weeks ago."

Ida just cackled.

"*Anyway*," Bev huffed, "Bathilda's the only one who might have a connection to Pigsend. But she's out of town, and Alice isn't sure when she'll be back. These guards gave me only a few days to find the real culprit before they're coming back for me."

"Oh dear, Bev. You really have got yourself in a bind this time," Ida said with a shake of her head.

"Not intentionally," Bev said. "But my goose is cooked if I don't figure this out soon."

"What was Bathilda hoping to sell to Lower Pigsend?" Ida asked.

"Let's say some livestock that wasn't on Her Majesty's approved list," Bev said. "She was looking to sell it quickly with all the soldiers in town."

"And nobody else in Pigsend knew about them?" Ida asked.

"Nobody—" Bev stopped, an idea popping into her mind. "Wait. Someone else *did* know about them." She broke into a grin. "You're a genius, Ida. Thank you!"

"You're welcome?" Ida called as Bev dashed out the door.

~

Mayor Hendry had purchased some of Bathilda's tanddaes wool to be made into a tunic for herself—and though it was a long shot that the mayor knew who Bathilda had sold to, it was worth a conversation. Especially since Bev didn't have anything else.

The mayor's office was in the large town hall in the center of Pigsend. The scaffolding for Ramone's statue was in place, but the actual rock was nowhere to be seen.

She pushed open the door. The town hall was quiet and empty, but lights were burning in two rooms facing each other. A smile came to her face—Sheriff Rustin must've come back to town. He'd been gone for a few weeks, on holiday, so Bev had heard, and although he didn't do much enforcing of the law or helping solve the mysteries around Pigsend, it was still nice to have him back.

"Hey there, Sheriff," Bev said, walking into his office.

The large, blond, blue-eyed sheriff jumped, staring at Bev as if she were a ghost. "Oh, it's just you, Bev. Goodness gracious, you scared me half to death."

"Sorry about that. Thought I was walking loudly enough to be heard," Bev said. "Welcome back. How was your trip? Were you on holiday for the winter?"

He scoffed and looked quite put out, a new expression for him. "Holiday! I wish."

"What happened?"

"Well, right after Dag Flanigan showed up, I was summoned back to Queen's Capital. They were very interested in all the *things* happening in town. I told them they all had perfectly reasonable explanations —and had to tell about fifty different committees the same things."

"I do hope you also told them that *several* of the things, as you put them, were caused by the queen's own people," Bev said with a look.

"I'm not *stupid*, Bev. I'm not about to point fingers at the people who'd have me sacked for questioning them," he said with a laugh. "But I did my best. I wasn't sure they'd let me go without sacking me anyway, but they did. So now I'm back and on *probation*, whatever that means." He sighed. "I just hope there's no more funny business for a while. I hear a bunch of destruction happened in town while I was gone. Did you ever figure out what it was?"

"I believe Mr. Flanigan said it was a dragon shifter," Bev said. "But it must've moved on, because we haven't had any excitement in weeks."

"Good," he sniffed. "Flanigan. Hope I never have to cross paths with him again."

"Likewise." Bev laughed. "Well, I was just coming to say welcome home. Glad to have you back."

"Glad to *be* back." He broke into a smile. "But who else wants to come live here in the farmlands.

Karolina Hunter? Hardly."

Bev bade him farewell and crossed the hall to Mayor Hendry's office. The mayor had very pale skin, blood red lips, and black hair. She was preternaturally pretty and always put together, even buried in concentration as she read through town papers.

"There aren't any falling buildings or sinkholes or other mysteries, to my knowledge," Hendry said, not looking up. "So I can't *imagine* why you're here, Bev."

"Can't it be a social visit?"

Hendry dropped the paper an inch and gave her a look.

"I have a question about…Bathilda," Bev said, taking a seat in one of the new chairs Earl had finally finished. "If you'll recall our last conversation about her."

"Mm." She leaned to the side and called across the town hall. "Rustin, dear?"

"Yes, ma'am?" In his office, he popped up to stand as if she'd commanded it.

"Can you run down to Etheldra's and see what kind of sweets Allen baked today?" She flashed a winning smile. "I'm feeling like a cookie."

"You got it!" Almost immediately, he jumped to his feet and ran out the door. After a moment, Hendry turned to Bev and smiled.

"How often do you use magic on him?" Bev

asked.

Hendry, who'd very recently confessed to being able to manipulate people's thoughts and actions with magic, just snorted. "My dear, have you met Rustin? I don't need to use magic."

"Fair."

"Now." She sat back. "What in the world do you want?"

"Have you heard of Lower Pigsend?" Bev asked.

"The place where all Her Majesty's naughty creatures have sought refuge?" She flashed a smile. "Of course I've heard of it. It's practically down the street."

"Down being the operative word," Bev said. "I'm surprised you know about it, considering—"

"The talisman that keeps it safe from the queen's people?" Another white smile. "Bev, really, you must give me more credit. It's my job to know these things."

"So I see."

Hendry lifted her porcelain chin. "What do you want with Lower Pigsend?"

"Well, that talisman you mentioned...someone stole it recently," Bev said. "And they think it was someone who used Merv's tunnel. Well, they suspect *me*, but goodness knows I don't need anything else magical in my life."

"Someone *stole* the talisman?" Hendry said, actually looking concerned. "Surely, they have some real suspects. Merv wouldn't be so careless."

"He did leave his tunnel open, but nobody knows about it," Bev said. "Well, nobody except me, Ida, and Allen."

"Goodness me. Who do they suspect?"

"Me, for one, but they didn't find the talisman at the inn," Bev said. "I was hoping to speak to Bathilda about who she was coordinating with to sell her tanddaes, but she's out of town."

"Yes, that sale netted her quite the treasure," Hendry said.

"Do you know who she sold them to?" Bev said.

"I don't know anything more than that they were sold," Hendry said, and looked honest about it.

"Well, there goes my only lead." Bev sank in the chair. "And perhaps mine and Merv's freedom."

"Don't be so dramatic," Hendry said. "Surely, you have something else to go on?"

Bev shook her head. "I told the two *lovely* guards who showed up at my door—"

"They showed up at your door?" Hendry said, tilting her head in confusion. "*How?*"

"What do you mean?"

"No one's supposed to be able to go in or out," Hendry said. "At least, that was my understanding. How did they get out?" She paused. "And how did you get *in?*"

"Merv's tunnel," Bev said. "He said he somehow

dug around the talisman."

She chuckled. "That's supposed to be impossible. From what I understand the magic to be, it was supposed to completely enclose the community. Nobody in, nobody out." She paused. "Which does beg the question..."

"Who was that man?" Bev finished for her.

She sat back and steepled her fingers. "If I were you, I'd start by asking if anyone's brought a herd of tanddaes in from somewhere. Last I saw, Bathilda had nearly twenty-five of them—that's not something you can just *sneak* into town without attracting some interest."

Bev nodded. "Do you think whoever she sold them to would flaunt them in public like that?"

"Perhaps not, but small towns...they have a way of sharing information." She pulled the paper up in front of her face again. "But just remember, Bev, you're Pigsend's first. I can't have you disappearing to the below-ground worlds when we have our own problems to deal with."

Bev started. "Do we have any problems right now?"

"Well, not at the moment, but you never know when a dead body might show up under mysterious circumstances."

Chapter Seven

Two more guests came to stay at the Weary Dragon that night, none of whom merited even a half-hearted sniff from Mr. Biscuit. No one from Lower Pigsend darkened her door, threatening arrest, so Bev hoped that Nog and Bola had found the talisman, and all was well. But she had a sneaking suspicion that wasn't the case.

The next morning, she finished her chores early, said goodbye to her guests, and headed toward Merv's to check on him. Allen's pastry of the day was sweet cheese-filled buttery bread, and she thought it would be just the thing to cheer Merv up.

The tunnel was still open to anyone who knew about it, something Bev thought was a bit dangerous, given the circumstances. But she was pleased she could make the trek to see her friend. The lanterns were burning on the outside of his home, and Merv was visible through the front windows. When he opened the door, she was doubly relieved to find Lillie, a basket of goodies on the table. At least Merv had one good friend left.

"Bev, oh goodness!" Merv exclaimed. "Have you heard the ghastly news? What they're thinking of doing to me?"

"Calm down, Merv, they aren't going to take you away," Lillie said. "They're just trying to scare you."

"Well, they've succeeded!" He sat and began furiously knitting the ball of green yarn. "Do you think they'd let me take my yarn with me to prison?"

"I think it's premature to consider that," Lillie said. "Bev, surely you can talk some sense into him. I've been trying all morning, but I don't think I'm doing much good."

"I can't say I'd be much help," Bev said. "I was visited by two of your lovely guards. They searched my inn the other night and threatened to arrest me, too."

"Oh, Bev!" Merv wailed. "How foolish of me to get you wrapped up in this! I should've known. Things aren't like they used to be, for sure. Everyone's on edge now. Nobody's safe!"

Bev was inclined to agree that it had been quite foolish of him to bring her into town, especially considering the strictness with which they protected their city from outsiders. But he was already in such a state, it didn't feel like it would be helpful to point that out.

"Let's not give up hope quite yet," Bev said. "There's at least one other person who knows of Lower Pigsend and promised to sell something there. Bathilda's tanddaes buyer, if you recall."

Merv sniffed loudly, dabbing his small eye with a knitted blanket. "You're right! I completely forgot about that."

"The tanddaes are gone, and I believe you would've heard the lot of them walking through your house if they'd come down this way," Bev said. "Which leads me to believe there must be some other tunnel people are using."

"Are you serious?" Lillie said, her eyebrows raising into her blonde curls. "Oh, the magistrate won't like that."

"I mentioned it to Officers Nog and Bola the night before last, and told them I'd find them a name," Bev said. "And I went to ask Bathilda the name of the person she'd sold the sheep to, but she's been on holiday for a month."

"I bet you could ask someone at the Merchant's House," Lillie said thoughtfully. "There's a livestock manager there. He'd surely have seen a herd that size walk through."

"Do you think it would've raised some eyebrows?" Bev asked. "A herd arriving from seemingly nowhere?"

"I can't say," she replied with a shake of her head. "It's such a busy place, you know."

"I don't know if it's a good idea for me to go back to Lower Pigsend," Bev said. "Might cause a stir if I do. Or Nog and Bola might decide I'm better off in jail."

"I doubt if twenty people know about you," Lillie said. "I'd wager they're trying to keep it under wraps as much as possible. There'd be mass hysteria if the townsfolk knew about Merv's tunnel to the surface."

"Well, shouldn't we close it, then?" Bev asked.

Merv let out a mournful wail. "I couldn't bear it! You're too dear a friend, Bev. To never see you again?"

"Besides that," Lillie said, "if what you say about the tanddaes is true, then there's another tunnel somewhere. Closing Merv's won't accomplish anything."

"I suppose that's true," Bev said. "What I can't figure out is who would want to take the thing protecting them from the queen's people?"

"Not everyone who lives in Lower Pigsend was hunted by Her Majesty," Lillie said. "Plenty of regular humans who sought refuge during the war ended up stuck after the spell was cast. I'm sure they'd have no problem walking up to the upside and going on their merry way."

"Got anyone in particular in mind?" Bev asked.

"Too many to count," Lillie said. "For every ten magical creatures running from the queen, there's a regular person without any magic to speak of."

"What about the moment it was taken? Were there any witnesses? What was happening?"

"If there were, I doubt Bola and Nog would tell you about them," Lillie said. "If you ask me, they're content to blame Merv and that's that."

"Certainly not," Bev said. "The magistrate is keen to uncover the truth, aren't they?"

"They're keen to keep the peace," Lillie said with a frown. "Bev, if we're going to clear Merv's name, we need to find this tunnel."

Bev sighed. Getting embroiled in another mystery was the last thing she wanted to do, especially one so far from the Weary Dragon. But if Lillie was right, and the local authorities would blame Merv for something he had nothing to do with, Bev had no choice but to see this through.

"Very well," Bev said. "I think we start with this Merchant's House and the tanddaes."

"You're a true friend, Bev." Merv wiped his small eyes with the tip of his claws. "Thank you. Oh, thank you!"

"I'll take you," Lillie said. "I've got to get back

to the bakery, too." She patted Merv on the shoulder. "Now, Merv. You need to eat these cookies. I added a little calming magic to them to ease some of your anxiety."

"You can do that?" Bev asked with brows raised.

"Well, it's not quite as potent as someone who has a lot of magic," Lillie said, blushing a little. "But I can do a little manipulation here and there. Calming and relaxation are my specialties. Comes with the cozy aspect of my magic."

Bev nodded and put her hand on Merv's shoulder. "Will you be all right, Merv?"

"As long as I've got my two dear friends to help me, I surely will be." He picked up a cookie and plopped it in his mouth. "And these amazing—" His head dropped as a loud snore came from his lips.

"Huh. Might've overdone it on the calming magic," Lillie said with a wince. "But he seemed in such a state, I wanted to make sure he got a bit of rest."

"I'm sure he'll appreciate it when he wakes up," Bev said.

~

Lillie led Bev down the tunnel into Lower Pigsend, which Bev approached with much more trepidation than the first time. She expected to see a sentry or guard or some kind of barrier keeping people out of the tunnel, but there wasn't one.

"Clearly, they aren't *that* concerned if they're leaving Merv's tunnel unguarded," Bev said.

"Well, the spell is still in effect," Lillie said.

"How do you know?" Bev asked.

"Well, because whatever door you walked through to get to Merv's living room...I couldn't see," she said.

Bev frowned. "What do you mean?"

"I'm not exactly sure how it works," she said. "But you kind of just...appeared to me. I assume you walked through a door because I heard knocking. But to my eyes, it's a blank wall. I assume it's the same for those who can't pass through to Lower Pigsend."

Bev nodded slowly. That certainly explained why the queen's soldier she'd brought to Merv's hadn't asked to continue down the tunnel. It was quite ingenious, she had to say.

"But I assume once the spell is broken, both doors will be visible to everyone," Lillie continued. "And, as I said, I'm convinced they're willing to let Merv take the fall for their own incompetence with the magistrate."

Inside the city, Lillie made a beeline for her bakery, saying she needed to check on some things she'd left in the oven.

"You're confident enough to leave your baked goods in the oven?" Bev asked.

"Well, that's part of the pobyd magic," she said.

"I can cast a spell on them to prevent them from burning. Won't last forever, of course, but if I find myself unexpectedly detained, I can usually get a bit of grace from it."

"That would certainly be a skill I'd like to have," Bev said. "You can't imagine how often I'm tied up with this or that and my bread comes out by the skin of its teeth."

"It's been a long time since I've baked bread," she said with a sigh. "Do you have a root cellar or something like that? You could always put it down there to give yourself a bit more time."

Bev started. "Really?"

She nodded. "It slows down that first bulk proof. Best would be to put it on ice, but I doubt that's available to you up there."

"No," Bev said with a shake of her head. "Lillie, I'm so happy we met."

"Me too." She grimaced. "I just wish it was under less dire circumstances."

Bev tutted. "Poor Merv. Do you think he'll be all right?"

"I think he'll be better if we can find out who really took the talisman. I—" Her eyes widened. "What in the *world*...?"

The front door to Lillie's bakery was open, and Officer Nog was inside, ransacking the place.

"Stop! Stop this instant!" she exclaimed, dashing toward her store with Bev right behind her. "This is beyond the pale, Nog! You won't find the talisman in my bakery. What in the world do you think you're doing?"

"We've reason to believe the talisman is still in Lower Pigsend. I'm searching the whole town." Nog had turned over a bag of nut flour, and was unceremoniously stomping through it, leaving a trail of crumbs on the floor as he peered inside cabinets and threw pastries on the floor. "No exceptions."

"Search if you must, but do you have to destroy my shop?" She ran over to the bag of flour and pulled it upright as carefully as she could. "This took me a whole day of grinding to make."

"The moleman and his above-ground accomplice were here the day they..." He trailed off, noticing Bev. "Well, isn't this convenient? You've saved me a trip."

"Thought I would've seen you yesterday if you wanted to talk to me," Bev said, looking around the shop. "You said the talisman is still in Lower Pigsend? How do you know?"

"Doesn't matter how I know," he huffed as he ran his fingers through a large bag of walnut flour. "I just do."

"So if it's still here, are you saying you're leaving me and Merv alone?" Bev asked. That would certainly save her a few headaches. "After all, if there's no crime..."

"There certainly *was* a crime! That mole broke a

hole in our protective spell and opened a door *anyone* could just walk through," he snarled, glaring at Bev.

"And apparently, someone else did the same thing," Bev replied with a look.

He let out a low grunt. "You're supposed to be finding me that person, if memory serves. You got a name yet?"

"Not yet," Bev said. "But I'm working on it. My one lead seemed to have skipped town."

"Well, that's convenient."

"Not really, as she had the answers I was looking for," Bev said. "So I'm trying a different tack. But it seems this is the sort of thing you and your partner should be doing." She paused, not seeing him. "Where is he, anyway?"

"Bola is off searching for a replacement talisman," Nog said, looking inside the now-empty cabinet before leaving the doors open. "Since we've been *so far* unable to locate the missing one."

"Then perhaps you can look into this herd of tanddaes and let me get back to my inn," Bev said.

"I'm busy." He flung another cupcake to the ground, earning a cry of angst from Lillie.

"This stuff's not easy to come by, you know," Lillie said with a glare as she yanked the bag away from him. "Costs me three gold coins for the wizard to replicate the bushels of walnuts, and a whole day of grinding to turn it into flour. And you've tossed it on the floor like it's nothing."

He snorted. "Looks like there's nothing to be found here. But I've got my *eye* on you, baker. If I catch this topsider bringing you anything illegal—"

"You'll have my head, I hear you," Lillie said, making a face as she gathered the destroyed sweets in her hands. "As long as it doesn't involve you throwing my wares on the floor again. This is going to take me all day to clean up."

"Then perhaps you shouldn't be hanging out with this topsider," Nog said, before turning to Bev. "You've got until Bola returns to find me this mythical second tunnel, or that moleman is going to be in a world of hurt."

"And when will that be?" Bev asked.

"Who knows?" He waddled toward the door. "And don't let me catch you getting in my way, either."

The door slammed behind him. "Wouldn't dream of it," Bev said, lightly. "Goodness, is he always so…"

"Yes, and he's gotten worse over the last few years," Lillie said, scooping the walnut flour with her hands and putting it into a large bin. "I know the magistrate wants to keep the town safe from the queen, but overzealous seems an apt description now."

"He didn't seem interested in hearing about another tunnel," Bev said. "For that matter, how did *he* get to the inn? Do you think he knows about the tunnel?"

"Probably. And he doesn't want you to find out." Lillie grabbed a broom and swept up the mess of icing, sponge, and sugar art Nog had left on the floor. "I can't believe he was so careless. These took me ages to make. Going to take me at least a week to remake them all."

Bev sighed, her heart going out to the baker. "What a mess."

"You said it," Lillie said, looking around the destroyed shop. "I'm so sorry, Bev. But I've got to stay here and remake all this flour and these pastries. Everything's got to go in the bin."

"Everything?" Bev frowned.

"Everything. Don't know what his grubby little fingers touched." She made a face as she picked up what appeared to Bev to be a mostly intact cupcake.

"Let me bring that to my laelaps," Bev said, taking it from her. "At least someone will get to enjoy it."

"Are you heading back, then?" Lillie asked.

Bev glanced at the clock on the wall. She still had a few hours. "No, I think I should continue on. Made it all the way down here, after all. It didn't seem too difficult to find the Merchant's House yesterday."

"Just keep walking toward the center of town," Lillie said. "It has a habit of just showing up, no matter how many wrong turns you make." She frowned a little. "Just be careful. You saw how zealous Nog is about keeping the town safe. If someone's smuggling things into town, they'd probably want to keep it under wraps, you know? No telling what they'd do to someone who'd expose them."

Bev nodded. "I'll do my best to keep my nose clean."

Lillie brightened. "Oh, who am I talking to? Of course, you've done this sort of thing before. I'm sure you know exactly what to do."

Chapter Eight

Bev wasn't sure about Lillie's vote of confidence, but she set off for the Merchant's House anyway. There did seem to be a different air in the town now, with fewer people strolling the streets, and those who were out seemed to carry their worry on their faces. Bev felt for them—they'd considered themselves safe all this time, and now they might have nowhere else to go.

The question of *who* would do such a thing hung in her mind. Unlike the mysteries in Pigsend, Bev was working at something of a disadvantage. She didn't know the people or the rules in Lower Pigsend. Didn't understand half the magic that kept this place running. She would've much preferred to have Lillie by her side as she approached the Merchant's House, lest she make some sort of faux pas and reveal herself to be a—what did they call it? Topsider?

The Merchant's House was reminiscent of the Pigsend town hall building, with a large spire out front bearing a clock and white wooden siding. But there was something ominous about it, and as Bev drew closer, it actually seemed to grow in size until it dwarfed everything around it. Perhaps *three* Pigsend town hall buildings could fit inside it, if Bev had to guess.

The two front doors were impossibly tall but light as a feather as Bev pushed them open. A burst of conversation hit her ears and she was overwhelmed by the sound for a moment before the rest of her caught up.

Lower Pigsend was markedly more populated than the town Bev inhabited—but inside this town hall, the busyness was exacerbated by the number of creatures crammed into the space, a thousand conversations happening at once. It was hard to know where to look, from the small dormice having squeaking conversations with a pair of pointy-eared, winged sparkly creatures to the three large tree-like men whose heads scraped the top of the ceiling even as they hunched over and pointed at barrels that they picked up and drank in one fell swoop. Unlike the worried neighbors on the streets, everyone here seemed more interested in their business than the outside world encroaching on it.

"Goodness me." Bev put her hand on her head. It certainly *would* be easy to sneak something from Pigsend in here.

"Pork, fed with magically replicated acorns!"

"Cotton! Magically replicated cotton for your shirts and tunics!"

"Get your potatoes here! Straight from the ceiling to your dinner table."

"Next, please. Next! Hurry, hurry, we haven't got all day."

Bev's attention was drawn to a scowling young man with a clipboard. He seemed perpetually tired as he looked at his clipboard and back at the people queued up. One had scraps of fabric, another had an empty wagon with a single vase inside, another carried several bags of something Bev couldn't quite make out.

"Yes, what do you have?" the clipboard-man said.

"Two bags of almonds." He lifted the bag for inspection. "Looking for at least ten to sell at market today."

Clipboard sniffed the bags and poked at them. "Magically sourced?"

"Nope. All original."

Clipboard pulled a long wooden stick from behind the clipboard and tapped it against the bags.

They shivered and shimmied and shrank and grew before settling back into their seller's hands.

"Five bags is all we can do today. That'll be a gold."

The merchant grumbled but paid the man then marched through a large open door that led to an antechamber off the main room. Bev tilted her head but couldn't see beyond the velvet curtains. But not a few moments later, the seller reemerged with five bags in addition to his original two. He nodded his cap to Clipboard, who didn't notice as he was inspecting another person's goods.

"Yes, yes, all original. Been saving it for a rainy day, but all my clothes are becoming threadbare." The woman had purple skin and a small dragon perched on her shoulder. She had a bolt of fabric that he was inspecting, but based on the disgruntled look on his face, the news wasn't going to be good.

"We can't do much with hemp, you know that," Clipboard said. "But if you'd like to risk it, it'll be a silver to get another bolt of fabric."

"Worth it," she said, placing the silver in his hand. "Don't like the feel of wool. Scratchy. And the tanddaes wool messes with my magic too much."

Bev started. *Did she say tanddaes?*

The woman disappeared into the antechamber as the other man had done, but when she emerged, she had nothing in her hands. Clipboard gave her a look that said "told you so" before turning back to the customer in front of him.

Bev hopped to her feet and followed the woman. "Excuse me!"

She turned, glaring at Bev. "What?"

"You mentioned tanddaes wool." Bev offered a smile. "Where might I find some?"

The woman scoffed, as if Bev were asking what color the sky was. "Right behind you. Of course."

Bev turned in the direction she'd pointed, among the merchants hawking their wares.

There! The purple color was unmistakable.

"Wool! Wool from a tanddaes! Perfect for your cozy blankets, tunics, and socks!"

She walked up to him with a smile on her face. Someone had snapped up the tanddaes wool quickly, and they were finalizing the details as Bev approached.

The man had two small horns coming out of his forehead and gave Bev a once-over before stuffing the gold coins into his pocket. It was a fraction of what Bathilda had been paid when she'd sold the creatures, but if one was merely shearing off the wool, a tidy profit could be made quickly.

"Excuse me," Bev said.

"I'm all out," he snapped, not even looking at her. "Come back later."

"Where did you get the tanddaes?" Bev asked.

He stopped, his beady eyes finally sweeping up

toward her. "Who's asking?"

"Me," Bev said with a firm smile. "I was wondering if—"

"If you have questions, you'd better have gold to pay for the answers. Otherwise, I've got work to do." And before Bev could say a word, he disappeared into the ether with a *pop*.

"Was he…?" Bev had seen that sort of behavior before, with a creature called a barus. But that small man had seemed to be a similar species. Then again, one look around the room told Bev she was woefully inept at identifying magical creatures.

"Pardon."

Bev spun around and, for a moment, couldn't identify who'd spoken. Until she tilted her head down to take in a large frog-like creature, barely up to her hips. He cast a wide grin at her and adjusted his straw hat, which was odd, considering there wasn't any sunlight down here.

"I'm sorry, what did you say?" Bev said, too taken aback by the sight of him to hear what he'd said.

"I said, were you looking for the tanddaes pen?" He adjusted his suspenders. "I'd be happy to take you there. It's just this way."

"S-sure," Bev said. "Lead the way."

He hopped forward, his hat somehow staying on his head as he moved across the room. Clearly, he was adept at navigating the crowded space (or the crowd was used to him), because he managed it without knocking anyone over. Bev followed him to the edge of the room and through a pair of open barn doors into a much larger space beyond.

Would anything in this place cease to amaze her?

As far as the eye could see, large pens were filled with every different kind of animal one could think of—and a few Bev couldn't. To be sure, there was a pen for cows, pigs, goats, and chickens, but between were unicorns, creatures with the head of a lion and the body of a bull, and something that looked like a cross between a duck and a cat. Of course tanddaes wouldn't be interesting with all these other creatures floating about.

"We have an auction every other Tuesday," he said. "Roughly around one, but you know, some of the morning ones go long or short, so it's always best to be here early if you've got your heart set on them. They go for anywhere from twenty to fifty gold coins, depending on the day. Just have to really wait for a time when no one else is looking, but I'm sure you knew that."

"Mm." Bev's gaze landed on a unicorn with a rainbow-colored tail, and it took her a moment to pull herself away. "How often do you get new ones in?"

"Oh, all the time. Here we are!" He gestured one webbed hand toward the pen. "Most of the ones who were born during the last breeding season have just come of age, so we've had a large influx lately. As I said, we'll be having an auction this upcoming Tuesday, but you're welcome to take a look at any that catch your fancy."

Bev's heart sank. Bathilda's flock had numbered roughly twenty. Perhaps two hundred bleated and chomped on hay in the pen beyond. Which had been Bathilda's and which were from someone else was anyone's guess.

"Is this all of them?" Bev asked, hoping to buy some time.

"You need more?" He chuckled. "Better have a load of gold on you—and then some! These things eat more potato skins than the cows and goats combined. Barely make a profit on them with all I have to pay the wizard."

"Did you get any from Upper Pigsend?" Bev asked.

He let out a loud guffaw of laughter. "Upper Pigsend? Well, I suppose the original herd came from up there, for sure." He paused, rubbing the back of his slimy head. "Not quite sure what it is you're asking?"

Bev hesitated, then decided to just come out with it. "I'm looking for a herd of twenty-five that arrived a few weeks ago from Upper Pigsend. Someone sold them to a gent from down here, and —"

Directness was clearly not the way to go, because

the frogman's eyes narrowed into slits. "Who did you say you were?"

"No one. Just curious." She took a step back and inched toward the main house again. "Thanks for the chat!"

~

Bev wasn't about to stick her neck out in a situation she didn't have any context for, but it was enough that she'd made him suspicious. Did he know part of his flock *had* come from Upper Pigsend? Or had some mysterious middleman procured them and told him not to ask questions?

The clock on the wall said Bev needed to head back to the inn to tend to things there, but she couldn't bring herself to leave just yet. Not when she had a feeling Nog would be back knocking on her door when he finished ransacking all the good businesses in town.

But it seemed an impossible ask. She had no idea where to go, who to ask, what was out of the ordinary. Someone like Lillie would be much better suited to look into this, and Bev could be back at the inn where she belonged. But Lillie had her own business to run, and—

Bev was so distraught, she didn't notice where she was going until she ran into the back of something tall, broad and...*feathery?*

"Pardon me," he said, his beak moving strangely as it formed words.

"P-pardon..." Bev said, watching him walk away.

He wore no clothes, but then again, his feathers were so thick, perhaps he didn't need to. His legs were bare, leathery almost, and his feet were clawed like a chicken's. In fact, he looked more like a chicken than anything else, except he was bright yellow.

He walked up to a man with a pig snout who had several buckets of plants at his feet.

"What can I do for you today, Mr. Rickshaw?" asked the pig.

Bev started. *Rickshaw?* There was a Rickshaw up in Pigsend. Bernard Rickshaw, the apothecary. But he certainly wasn't a half-chicken.

"Just need some mint, propolis, and weatherwood root today. Fresher, if you've got it, but magically replicated is fine, too," the yellow-feathered man said, looking inside the pots.

The pig began scooping the dried herbs into small bags he had on hand. "Things good at the apothecary shop?"

Apothecary? Now things were past coincidental. Bev inched closer.

"Quite well. Though things seem to be a bit busier than usual. Everyone's got their feathers in a twist with this talisman missing." He rubbed a feathered wing against his head. "Got ten new orders for people stocking up in case they have to leave quickly."

"You don't seem worried," the other man said.

"I got some things brewing," he said with a knowing look. "Might just relocate back to Pigsend."

The other man laughed. "Looking like that?"

"Well, maybe." Another knowing look. "I know my brother wouldn't be happy to see this feathered face in his shop."

Brother? Could this bird man be related to Bernard?

"Oh, I didn't know you had a brother?"

"Yeah, runs the apothecary in Pigsend. Probably into the ground by now. Man never did have much sense."

"Yeah, I used to live in Middleburg myself," said the other man. "Had a thriving wand-making business. Wonder what happened to the old building, you know?" He chuckled. "I'm sure it's been taken over by someone else. Times change and people move on."

"That they do. See you around, John."

They parted ways. Bev couldn't help but follow the birdman. Not that having a brother in Pigsend, and one that Bev knew, was in any way helpful to her cause, but she couldn't help her curiosity. Bernard had never mentioned a brother to her, but so many in Pigsend had things they didn't like to talk about.

In the crowded room, it was easy for Bev to keep an eye on the brightly colored feathers. The apothecary stopped at a few more places, picking up ingredients for tinctures and chatting with the merchants. Finally, he waved goodbye to the last one and headed for the door.

Bev waited until he was back on the street before she called out to him. "Excuse me!"

He stopped, turning and smiling at her—which was odd, considering he had a beak. "Yes? Can I help you?"

"I…uh…" Goodness, how was she supposed to go about this? Might as well just come out with it. "Sorry for overhearing, but did you say your name was Rickshaw?"

He nodded and brightened. "Gerry Rickshaw, at your service."

"Are you…erm… Do you happen to be related to Bernard Rickshaw, of Pigsend?"

His eyes—which seemed oddly human—lit up in recognition, and he seemed happy to discuss the topic now. "My dear brother! You know of him?"

Bev nodded. "Perhaps not common knowledge, but I live in Pigsend. Well, the one up there. I—"

"Oh, you're the one Nog's in a tizzy about? The one he claims stole the talisman?" He chuckled, and Bev got the distinct impression Gerry wasn't worried about the missing talisman at all.

"He's claiming that?" Bev frowned. "I would've

thought he wouldn't have said anything."

"Well, that was the *first* story, that some topsider had snuck into town and snatched it. But when he didn't find it, he changed his tune and said someone in town stole it. Was in my shop earlier today making a mess of things." He shook his head. "You know how those magistrate officers are."

"Uh-huh," Bev said. "Clearly not interested in finding the truth, are they?"

"Well, it wasn't me, if that's what you're asking," Gerry said with a huff. "Not as if I could sneak anywhere with these feathers. Everyone can see me from halfway across town."

Bev couldn't argue with that logic. "Actually, I wasn't stopping to ask if you were the culprit. I was being nosy, and wanted to know if you were related to Bernard." She paused, eyeing him. "You said you were…brothers?"

He let out a deep chuckle. "I didn't *always* look like this. Why don't you come with me to my shop, and we can talk more?"

Chapter Nine

Gerry's shop was a tidy little two-story building with a front window filled with signs advertising different kinds of potions. Some were to help with healing, others relaxing, some boosted energy and one, probably very popular, was said to replenish the goodness of the sun.

"Welcome to my shop," he said, gesturing to the shelves and losing a few feathers. "Not sure how it compares to Bernie's, but—"

"Much larger, I'd say," Bev said, leaning down to inspect the items under the front counter. "And you've got many more different kinds of potions, for sure."

"Lots more folks down here, you know," he said.

"I was actually on my way back to Pigsend when the war broke out. I didn't want to chance running afoul of Her Majesty's preferred species, so I headed down here until the war was over. Then it was and…uh…" He gestured. "Well, then we all had to make the best of living down here. So here I am."

"And you've never gone back up?" Bev asked.

"Nobody has," he said. "We're all just living on magic and whatever we can scrounge from the earth. It's not my preferred way of living, I'll tell you that, but it's living, so it's better than the alternative."

Bev picked up a vial of turmeric tonic, reminded of what Lillie had said about people who were just trapped down here, and how they might have a motive to steal the talisman. Though she doubted a man with bright yellow feathers would be first in line to step into the sunlight.

"You're probably wondering about the feathers, hm?" He gestured to himself before plucking a few tinctures off the wall.

"It's not what I'm used to seeing," Bev said with a nervous smile. "You weren't always like this, you said? What in the world happened?"

"I'd go into the details, but I'm afraid it might bore you."

"I very much doubt that."

He lifted one of the vials. "Well, in apothecary school, I made a potion, and added the wrong ingredient—I think. You know, these recipes are so precise that the wrong thing or amount can have deadly consequences. But in my case, they just had *feathered* consequences." He laughed at his own joke. "Can't hide in a crowd, even if I wanted to. Always the center of attention."

Somehow Bev got the sense he didn't mind that. "Couldn't you make a potion to undo it?"

"Oh, yes. Was on my way to doing just that when the war broke out," he said. "Well, looking like this made the queen's people think there must be something unsavory about me. So I hid down here until cooler heads prevailed." He let out a sigh. "Still waiting, I suppose."

"And the wizard can't procure you the ingredients you need?" Bev asked.

He shook his head. "He's good, but not that good. Can't make something from nothing."

"Does he magically replicate the rest of your ingredients?"

"Yes, mostly," he said. "There are some things that do better than others. Mint does fairly well with the replication process, but you know it's darn near impossible to kill anyway." He ran his feathered hand along the counter. "I've done pretty well with what's available to me."

"I agree," Bev said. "You've got quite the shop for only being here five years. Bernard's been there for twenty, I believe."

"Longer! We were set to inherit the place.

Couldn't wait to go into business with my dear brother. But fate had other plans. I can't imagine what he'd say if he saw me looking like this." He turned to start mixing ingredients.

"With the talisman gone, you'll be able to go visit him, right?" Bev asked, hoping he might give up more information or some clue. "I'd be happy to tell him you're nearby."

He waved her off but didn't quite look her in the eye. "I'm sure they'll find the talisman, and everything will be right again. No use in getting ol' Bernard's hopes up just to dash them. I'm sure he's all but forgotten about his brother."

Bev opened her mouth to ask another question when the clock on the wall chimed loudly. Her heart dropped into her stomach. Was it *that late?*

"Goodness, I've got to be getting back," she said.

"Oh, that's right. *You* can come and go for some reason," Gerry said with a look Bev couldn't quite read. "Not sure how you lucked into that."

"You know, I'm not quite sure either," Bev said, walking toward the door. "I could perhaps bring you the ingredients you're missing to fix the potion. If they're not too difficult to find."

"As much as I appreciate that, if Officer Nog sees me walking around without my beak, he might get nosy about where it went."

"You're familiar with him as well?" Bev asked.

"He's in here every other week making sure I haven't gotten anything that the magistrate finds distasteful anyway. He's something of an ask-questions-later sort of fellow."

"So I've noticed," Bev said.

"Don't worry about me. I've got a few things brewing, so to speak." He winked.

~

Bev rushed through town, saying a quick hi and goodbye to Merv as she hurried through his house then up the tunnel and out into the bright afternoon. Without the sun to remind her of the time, she'd allowed herself to be distracted and waylaid. By now, her bread should've been on its second proof, she should've had her order in with the butchers already, and she prayed she hadn't had any guests stop by the inn and leave before she could get their reservation.

She was panting and sweating when she rushed into the butcher's shop, earning a quirked look from Ida.

"What in the world? Are you all right, Bev?"

"Fine, just..." She leaned on the counter. "Need to catch my breath."

"We were wondering where you'd run off to," Ida said. "Got a bit concerned, if I'm being truthful. You're never this late getting your order in."

"Lost track of time," she said, putting her hand to her chest. "Was down in...Lower Pigsend..." She straightened, taking a deep breath. "What do you have that'll be quick to cook?"

She went with a pork loin, hoping she could scrounge up some apples from the root cellar, and headed into the inn. Biscuit was more or less in the same spot she'd left him, but popped his head up to inspect her as she came bustling in. She put the meat down on the table and continued toward the cellar, Biscuit following. He put his paws up on her thigh and she patted him on the head.

"I'm fine," she said. "Just—"

He was nosing the pocket of her pants, where she'd kept the wrapped-up remnants of Lillie's cupcake that Nog had tossed on the floor. It seemed like ages ago she'd been in her bakery.

"Oh." She pulled out the smashed delicacy and unwrapped the paper. "Have—"

It was gone in two bites.

"Well, hope it was good."

She walked around the root cellar, taking stock of her flour stores. She had one half-empty ten-pound bag left, stamped with Sonny Gray's emblem, which would take her through another two or three days of loaf-making, especially if she didn't have a plethora of guests to feed.

But she was here to locate apples, so she pulled out crates to look for them—or something to serve with the loin. "Don't know what got into me. Ol' Wim would have my head if he knew I was gallivanting around in another town instead of keeping a close eye on his inn." In the second-to-last crate, she found a stash of apples, and she tossed them into her basket and brought them back to the kitchen.

But, of course, the moment she stepped inside, she was hit with the sense that it was *too cold* for that time of day. Her oven fires hadn't been set because she hadn't been there to set them.

"Oh, fiddlesticks," Bev said, pulling the towel off her rosemary bread. It certainly didn't look like it had doubled in size, even after the hours it had been sitting there. "Fiddlesticks, indeed."

The bread wasn't *mandatory*, per se, but she'd get an earful from Etheldra if it wasn't there. So she started the oven fires and shaped the dough anyway, hoping that she'd get the light, airy texture she was looking for at the end of it all.

All-in-all, she was rather proud of her scrambling and had somewhat salvaged her schedule. But then, just as she was putting the bread above the oven to proof, the front door opened.

"Bev?" Allen called. "Are you here?"

"Yes, coming," Bev said, wiping her hands.

"Where in the world have you been?" he said. "You had two guests come by today. They waited for over two hours, but when you didn't show, they said they were going to continue to Middleburg."

"They didn't look strange, did they?" Bev asked,

annoyed that she'd missed out on the gold.

"Strange how?"

"Never mind." She sank onto the stool by the kitchen table. "It's been a morning. I can't even begin to describe the things I saw down there."

"So you were in Lower Pigsend?" Allen asked. "Any progress on the investigation?"

"None. I'm somewhat out of my depth down there."

"Maybe you should hand the investigation off to someone else?" Allen asked. "Not to tell you how to do your business, but it's kind of hard to be in two places at once."

Bev sighed. "Merv is too dear a friend. Not to mention, I've got a hunch the town isn't quite as well-managed as I was led to believe. The guards who visited me seem to have their own agenda. First, they said I stole the talisman, then they said it was probably still in the village and were ransacking Lillie's bakery. And yet, they've left Merv's tunnel wide open."

"That seems…strange," Allen said.

"I can't make heads or tails of it myself. I can come and go. Lillie says she can't. The guards can come and go." She threw her hands in the air. "Something fishy is going on, but for the life of me, I don't have a clue what it could be."

"What's your next step?" Allen asked.

"If I can prove to someone, not quite sure who,

that there's another tunnel in town, maybe they'll leave Merv alone," she said.

"How are you going to do that?" Allen asked.

"I honestly don't know," Bev said, rubbing her face. "I got distracted by a large half-man, half-chicken, who happens to be Bernard's brother, by the way—"

"No." Allen straightened. "Gerry? Gerry is down there? Wow."

"What do you mean?"

"Well, Gerry and Bernard had something of a rivalry," Allen said with a chuckle. "It was like the Witzel brothers a few generations ago. They both wanted their parents' shop. Nobody's sure *exactly* what happened after they went off to study apothecary in a large university out west. But Bernard returned without saying a word about his brother and hasn't ever since."

"Huh." Bev rubbed her chin. "Well, I can tell you what happened to Gerry, in any case. Turned himself into half a chicken."

Allen shifted. "Come again?"

"A chicken," Bev said. "He's about this tall." She put her hand up to mark the height. "Covered in yellow feathers with claw-like feet. Supposedly, it was a potion gone wrong."

"Did *he* turn himself into a chicken, or did his brother?" Allen asked, suggestively wagging his eyebrows. "Maybe *he* stole the talisman to help change himself back!"

"Gerry said he did it to himself, and just lacks the proper ingredients to fix it," Bev said. "Don't you turn into Ida and make mountains out of molehills. Got enough mystery as it is."

"You did say you weren't sure what to do next," Allen said with a chuckle. "Maybe you pop down to Bernard's and ask about his brother."

Bev put her hands on her hips. "I really can't leave again. I already lost two customers today as it is."

"It's just down the street," Allen said. "I can keep an eye on things for you."

"That's very nice of you," Bev said.

"But only if you promise to tell me the entire sordid history when you get back," Allen replied with a grin.

~

The sun was getting lower in the sky as Bev walked into the apothecary shop. Bernard, a middle-aged, decidedly *human* man, was sweeping, but his face brightened when he saw her. Bev could almost see the resemblance between him and Gerry, even though one had a beak for a mouth.

"Bev!" Bernard said, walking to his front counter. "What can I do for you? Was just about to close for the day."

Bev figured she'd just come right out with it. "I had a question about your brother."

As predicted, Bernard's entire body went rigid, and his normally jovial eyes darkened considerably. "What about him?"

"Well, um… I hear he's nearby," Bev said.

"I'm sure you would hear it, considering he's made himself into a giant chicken." He returned to sweeping, albeit a lot more stiffly. "Or has he managed to undo his own medicine?"

"No, still a chicken," Bev said. "What in the world happened to him?"

Bernard put his broom away, and Bev thought she might be asked to leave, but instead he turned to her wearily. "Got too ambitious for his own good. We'd had a pact that we'd share the shop back here in Pigsend once our schooling was complete. But he wanted me out of the way, so he tried to slip me something in my breakfast."

"Oh, no!" Bev gasped. "Your own brother?"

He nodded. "It was the day before our graduation, and he brought me breakfast as a 'show of peace,' he said. But I'd never trusted him, not since we were young children and he tried to feed me a toad. He's never been *so* clever that he's been able to trick me, and he foolishly had the exact same pastry on his plate. So when he wasn't looking, I swapped them. Next thing I knew, he'd sprouted feathers."

"Was the intention to turn you into a half-chicken?" Bev asked.

"No. I think he meant to turn me into a full chicken, so he could keep me in a little pen outside the apothecary." He chuckled. "But as I said, he wasn't the cleverest of people. I thought it was a fitting punishment."

"Is there a cure?" Bev asked.

"I'm sure he's looked for one," Bernard said. "It's probably best suited for a wizard or mage to undo, with the complexity of it. But there don't seem to be many of those around lately, do there?"

Bev let out a nervous laugh. She *did* know where one was, and so did Gerry, which begged the question: why hadn't he gone to see the wizard to fix his problem yet? Was that the "thing brewing" he had planned? And if so, why not seek the cure sooner?

"And barring that, it would require a keen potion-making mind. Not something my brother possesses, unfortunately." He tilted his head. "Well? Does that answer your question?"

"Somewhat." Bev nodded. "Sorry to have bothered you with it. I've got to get back to finish up dinner, but I was just curious."

She turned to go when Bernard asked, with a sadder tone than Bev would've expected, "Is he very far?"

"Far enough," she replied after a moment. It perhaps wasn't the best course of action to tell everyone she came across about Lower Pigsend's existence. "He did mention you, somewhat...fondly, if that helps."

Bernard let out a low sigh. "He's my brother, but I still wouldn't trust him. Wyverns don't change their wings, as the saying goes." He nodded his head. "Have a good night, Bev."

"Thanks, Bernard."

Chapter Ten

Dinner was passable, though Etheldra was sure to comment that the bread wasn't up to Bev's usual standards. But as long as it was edible, it was okay. And although it wasn't great that she'd missed her possible guests, she didn't have to do laundry in the morning, so that was something of a silver lining. She didn't relish the idea of spending *another* day down in Lower Pigsend, but as she lay awake that night, staring at the ceiling with Biscuit snoring between her legs, she realized she'd probably have to.

She considered the day's events, from Merv's worry to Lillie's shop to the Merchant's House to Gerry and Bernard. The latter, she chided herself for, because it didn't seem pertinent to Merv's problem. Gerry might've tried to poison his brother, but that didn't mean he was capable of stealing a talisman. One that, by all accounts, was there to protect him as much as everyone else in town.

Besides that, she wasn't looking for the missing talisman. She assumed Nog and Bola had that covered, and they certainly were making a mess of things in their pursuit of it. No, her job was to prove that Merv wasn't the only one with a path to the upside, as they called it.

How, exactly, she was to do that remained something of a mystery.

Bev tossed and turned and plotted and thought and tried in vain to sleep. Around midnight, she was finally struck with an idea. The tanddaes idea had been a bust because they were common down there. But if she were to search for something that *wasn't* supposed to be down there, something not magical, that might be the way to go. Something like a sack of flour, which as Lillie said, couldn't be replicated by magic. If she could find that, that might lead her to who'd brought it to town, which could lead her to the second tunnel.

It was a very long shot, made more difficult by the fact that Bev didn't know what was supposed to be in the town and what wasn't. But hopefully, with Lillie's help, she'd be able to sort it out.

Then, of course, there was the larger problem of

the inn, and the job she was supposed to be doing. Morning came too soon, and even as Bev prepared her dough and ensured everything was ready, there was still a twinge of guilt at leaving her beloved inn unattended for another day. Allen would surely keep an eye on things, as would Ida and Vellora, but not having someone at the front desk didn't feel right.

"Well, not no one," Bev said, pulling on her traveling cloak as Biscuit wagged his tail at her feet. "You'll be here to keep an eye on things, won't you, Biscuit?"

He smiled at her, that unfailingly happy look on his face as he probably waited for her to feed him again.

"You know I'd take you," she continued, "but I'm afraid of what you'd do in the town. It would probably drive your little nose crazy."

He sat and tilted his head at her, as if trying to reason with her.

"I mean, *everything* is magical down there," Bev said. "You probably couldn't even get a few feet before you started chowing down."

He let out a low ruff.

"And the thing I'm looking for is, perhaps, *not* magical."

Ruff.

"Not the talisman," she said. "I mean, it would be nice to find that, too. But for now, I'm looking for something not touched by magic. Because it stands to reason that if I found something *not* magical, that's something that came from up here, not down there."

Ruff.

"And if I found something from up here down there, then I'd be one step closer to figuring out which passageway it came from, which gets me closer to finding the talisman," she finished, knowing full well it was insanity to talk with a dog, even one as expressive as her laelaps. She knelt and patted him on the head. "If I thought you could help, I'd bring you, but you're only good at finding magical things."

He nuzzled her hand and stared at her expectantly.

"Unless…" She stopped, blinking. "Well, that's a thought. Do you think you could find something in town that was made without magic?"

His tail wagged.

"Well, if you're sure." She stood. "Then…I suppose, let's go. But you leave Merv's blankets alone this time, understand? And don't you dare eat anything that Lillie doesn't offer."

Ruff.

~

Allen was the only one awake at this hour, and he was happy to keep an eye on things for Bev, though there was concern in his eyes when she told him she was going back down to Lower Pigsend.

But Biscuit nudged his way between her legs, and the baker relaxed a bit. Perhaps having a little backup wasn't such a bad idea, after all.

The trek to Merv's felt much longer than it had before, perhaps because Bev was making it for the third time in a week. Merv was, of course, awake when Bev knocked on his door, and he gave Biscuit a wary glance before allowing them entry.

"Just passing through," Bev said. "Biscuit's under strict orders to behave."

"That'll be hard for him, I reckon," Merv said, protectively putting one of his claws over the five new blankets he'd knitted in the past day. "Probably won't be able to control himself with all the magic down there."

"Well, that's kind of why I brought him this time," Bev said. "I thought if everything down there is touched by magic, Biscuit might be able to find something that *isn't*."

"Thus proving it came from Upper Pigsend?" Merv said with a slow nod. "Quite clever, Bev. You're getting good at this."

"Let's see if it pans out," she said. "I thought we might pop in to Lillie's first. See if she can spare a few hours to help us or at least point us in the right direction."

"She's a gem. Reminds me a lot of you," Merv said. "Smart. Capable. Big heart."

"I can tell," Bev said, hissing at Biscuit as his

pink nose strayed too close to the stack of blankets. "Well, we'll be on our way. Hopefully, I'll have some good news when I return in a few hours."

They continued toward Lower Pigsend, and the closer they came, the more Biscuit's tail perked up. Once again, there wasn't a guard, a barrier— nothing preventing Bev from coming and going as she pleased. It certainly made the accusations leveled against her and Merv lose their luster.

What in the world is really going on down here?

As predicted, Biscuit's tail wagged so fast it almost became a blur. He pressed his nose to the ground as he walked zigzags down the street, scaring the bits out of a pair of elves and causing another to jump up in fear. Bev apologized to both of them and grabbed Biscuit by the snout to look at her.

"Don't forget what we're here to do," Bev said. "We're looking for something *not* magic, remember?"

His pink tongue shot out and licked the tip of her nose.

She made a face and released his snout. "We're going to visit Lillie first and see if she has any updates. Can you hold it together until then?"

Biscuit stayed put, as if waiting for Bev to lead the way.

"Very good."

Lillie was inside her bakery, and waved at Bev as she walked inside. "Please tell me you've got good news for Merv." Her gaze dropped to Biscuit. "Oh! Who's this?"

"This is Biscuit, my d—my laelaps," Bev said, deciding it was probably okay to call him by his real name down here. She explained her plan to find a non-magical object, and Lillie clapped her hands in surprise.

"Bev, that's a brilliant idea," she said. "Though there *are* some things that aren't touched by magic. This potato, for example." She put it down to Biscuit's level, and the laelaps's tail didn't wag as he sniffed it. "Not magical."

"Anything else?" Bev asked.

"Root vegetables," she said, gesturing to the case. "Obviously. Rocks, dirt. Water—there's a small spring that feeds the rest of the town. But other than that…yes, I think most everything else is replicated by the wizard."

"Then we'll avoid the rocks and water and dirt," Bev said.

"Are you sure he can do this?" Lillie asked. "Laelaps are pretty headstrong."

Biscuit did a lap in the front of her shop. Bev thought he'd go straight for the confections, but he seemed to be searching for something else.

Lillie patted him, but he wriggled out of her grip, his nose leading him to the door. He pawed at it, letting out a low, expectant growl.

"Suppose he wants me to follow," Bev said with

a shrug. "Be right back."

Bev opened the door, and Biscuit dashed out, his nose to the ground and his tail pointed upward. Bev held her breath as they walked in the direction of the apothecary—was Gerry the culprit, after all?

But Biscuit walked right past the apothecary shop, down a left and a right until he sat in front of a door.

Ruff.

"What…." Bev tilted her head up to read the sign. *The Watering Hole.* "Is there something in here?"

Biscuit pawed at the door.

"Wait a minute. Beer is made with barley," Bev said, more to herself than to Biscuit. "And Lillie said grains don't stand up to magical replication. So how do they have beer here?"

Ruff.

"Good job, Biscuit," Bev said with a smile. "But if we go in there, I don't want you chomping down on anything you see. Let me have a conversation with them so I can understand what's going on, all right?"

Ruff.

With a deep breath, Bev opened the door, and was immediately hit by the scent of beer and yeast. It was familiar to her, as someone who brewed casks of beer for the patrons of the Weary Dragon, and the sight of the circular tables with several patrons eating what appeared to be breakfast made her a little homesick.

"Morning." The barkeep was a human-looking man with large glasses and no hair. "What are you having?"

"Oh, um…" Bev sat on one of the stools, and Biscuit obediently waited at her feet. "What do you have?"

"Potato gruel." He pointed to the large pot on the counter. "Beer'll have to wait until later this afternoon."

"Then gruel will be fine," Bev said. She'd been hoping to try the beer to compare it to hers and see if she could taste any magic.

"Getting an early start, are we?"

Bev jumped at the familiar voice, turning to find Officer Nog walking out of the shadows. She briefly feared he'd been following her, but he was carrying a bowl of gruel in his hand and had flecks of it on his misshapen mouth.

By her feet, Biscuit growled, and the officer shot him a dirty look.

"What'dya bring your filthy dog for?"

"He's helping me investigate. I don't suppose you're ransacking this place like you did Lillie's shop," Bev said. "Didn't you say you thought the talisman was still inside Lower Pigsend? Is that still your theory or are you working on a different one? And if the talisman is still inside Lower Pigsend, why are you threatening Merv? Is it because you want a scapegoat for your own failings?"

He worked his jaw, and a thrill of victory shot through her. "Our investigation is ongoing," he said, after a moment. "Which leads me to ask what *you're* doing here? Investigating the gruel? Lonny makes the best, if you're wondering."

"I was actually interested in the beer," Bev said.

"Thirsty?"

"I was curious how it compared to the brew I make at the Weary Dragon," Bev said. "Because I make mine with barley, and I was under the impression that's in short supply down here."

"Aye." Lonny chuckled. "Which is why when I need more, the wizard just replicates the beer, which does hold up to the spell."

Bev's hopes deflated. "Oh. I didn't know that."

"What you don't know could fill this whole cavern, lady," Nog said, walking up to her and poking her in the stomach. "I suggest you spend less time tasting the delicacies here and more time figuring out how to save your skins."

"Or," Bev said, "instead of antagonizing me at every turn, you could work with me, and we could figure this out together. I know there's another tunnel somewhere in this town, because I know a herd of tanddaes came from Pigsend to be sold down here."

Nog chuckled. "So sure of yourself, are you?"

"Well, then, answer me this: How come I can come and go?" Bev asked. "Why is it that the citizens of Lower Pigsend have to stay here, but I don't?"

Again, he worked his jaw, and Bev got the distinct impression he might've been throwing his weight around for no good reason.

"I wouldn't expect a topsider like you to understand how the magic works down here," Nog said, his green face coloring. "Don't you serve her a thing, Lonny. She's not welcome here. And just as soon as Bola returns with news on the replacement talisman, we'll be putting her behind bars."

That, too, seemed an odd parameter. "If you say so. C'mon, Biscuit, let's get out of here."

~

Biscuit protested, but Bev walked out of the tavern, feeling agitated and a bit ashamed that she'd wasted her time. Not only that, but she wasn't sure what to do now. Take Biscuit to Gerry's, perhaps? That seemed like another wild goose chase, but she *was* running out of time.

"Why did you take me there?" Bev asked Biscuit. "There wasn't anything worth finding."

Ruff.

"I'm serious. We don't have a lot of time to lollygag."

Biscuit seemed agitated, pawing at the ground and giving her a low growl.

"Don't be snippy with me," Bev said. "You're the one—Hey!"

He turned and took off down the street again. Bev threw her hands in the air but stormed after him. He left behind a little cloud of dust, so she was able to follow him down the street, then around the corner, then down a narrow alleyway between the buildings. There she found him standing atop what appeared to be a basement entryway. When she approached, he turned and scratched at the wooden doors furiously, as if there were one of Allen's delicious breakfast pastries beneath it.

"I can't..." Bev started then realized the door was unlocked. She checked the coast before opening the doors. Biscuit barely waited until they were open before scampering down the dark stairs. Bev, with a nervous inhale, followed.

There was a lingering scent of must in the air, and it was hard to see even a few feet in front of her, but Biscuit's white tail caught the scant light, so she followed it until it stopped. Her thighs hit something soft and heavy. Burlap. Then she smelled it—*barley*.

"Biscuit, is this...?" Bev began then her whole body went stick straight as the door above opened. She dove for cover, hiding behind the largest dark object she could see. Biscuit curled up next to her, his wide eyes reflecting in the dark. She craned her neck as a pinpoint light illuminated the space.

"Be right up, just need to check on tonight's brew."

Bev covered her mouth to quiet her gasp.

The light came closer, and she crouched as low as she could, hoping it wouldn't catch the tip of her hair or Biscuit's fur. But just before the light touched the edge of her boots, it turned away, as Lonny hovered over the large casks of beer. Bev chanced a peek, and her eyes widened as the light fell on the large, heavy, soft thing Biscuit had run into.

It wasn't just a bag of barley—it was barley with Sonny Gray's logo on it.

Chapter Eleven

Sonny Gray's unique logo was on every bag Bev had ever purchased from him. She'd seen it enough times to know it by heart—even in the scant light of the tavern basement.

She tried to temper her excitement. Although Lonny had clearly lied when he'd said his beer was magically replicated, that didn't mean his barley wasn't. Lillie hadn't mentioned barley specifically (although it was a grain), so maybe it was an exception. And Sonny's bag could've been down here when the spell was cast and was just being used to hold the grain that had been magically replicated. As Nog had said, what she didn't know could fill the cavern. Perhaps there was a perfectly reasonable explanation for all of it.

Or…it could be the lead she'd been looking for. After all, Lonny himself had said it was *beer* that was replicated, not barley. Bev knew the scent of brewing, and there was nothing magical about what was going on in those barrels.

Lonny finally finished messing with his casks, hoisted a crate onto his shoulder, and walked upstairs. Bev waited another five minutes before emerging from her hiding spot and creeping closer to the bags to inspect the contents. Biscuit's nose was pressed against her hands as she untied the bag, and she held her breath as barley came tumbling out into her hand. She put one in her mouth to taste it.

Certainly *tasted* like real barley.

There was a thud on the ceiling above, and Bev remembered she was sneaking around and should probably make her escape before she got caught. She scooped up a handful of barley kernels, stuffing them into her pants pocket before turning to Biscuit, who was nosing the remains of the barley on the floor.

"Let's go," she whispered.

They hurried up the stairs and out into the alley, Bev's head spinning the whole time as Biscuit kept at her heels. Once they were a safe distance away, Bev knelt and held out the barley for Biscuit to sniff.

"What do you think?" Bev asked. "Magical?"

His nostrils flared as he sniffed, but his tail

didn't wag.

"I'll take that as a no," Bev said, standing back up. "The better question is…how can we know for sure? And what do we do with this knowledge?"

Biscuit gave her a sideways look.

"Take it to Lillie?" Bev said after a moment. "Good idea. She'll know what to do."

Bev turned to walk toward the baker's shop when she once again almost ran into a large, yellow-feathered creature.

"Oh, hello, Bev!" Gerry said, steadying her as she teetered. "Fancy seeing you here!"

"Gerry, nice to see you again," Bev said with a tight smile. "Sorry about running into you. I don't know where my head was."

"No problem at all." He looked over her shoulder into the alley. "What were you doing down there?"

"A little lost," she replied, hoping she looked sincere. "Trying to make my way to Lillie's."

"The baker?" She nodded. "Love her. Love her cookies more. I should probably pop by and get myself a batch of those carrot-walnut delights."

Bev didn't love the idea of him walking with her, especially as she potentially had illegally sourced barley in her pocket, but she didn't want to be rude. "I'm happy to walk with you, if you'd like to go."

Thankfully, he shook his head. "No, I'm just on my way back from the Merchant's House. Got such a run on my goods lately. Everyone's preparing for the worst, you know. They all seem to think the queen's army's going to barge into town any day now." He sighed. "You're still looking for the talisman, aren't you?"

"Not the talisman," Bev said. "But if you know of any tunnels that go to the surface…"

"Other than the one you take?" He chuckled. "No, can't say that I do. But if you are looking into the talisman being missing, I wanted to share something I discovered. I was talking with Aaron who was talking with John who works over by the Merchant's House…"

Bev nodded as if she knew who any of those people were.

"And *they* say that when the talisman was stolen, there was some kind of big fuss happening. Apparently, everyone in the Merchant's House square began *sneezing*."

"Sneezing?" Bev said with a laugh. That hardly seemed worth talking about. "Maybe someone turned over a basket of something."

"Well, that's the thought. But it was so many people sneezing that it certainly drew enough attention that someone was able to walk right up to the talisman and take it without anyone seeing them."

"Do you think Officer Nog knows that?" Bev asked.

"Oh, I'm sure. They were all over it the moment the talisman disappeared," he said. "Said it was clearly some of Percival's magic gone wrong, but there's only so much they can lie to us about without us getting a bit suspicious."

Bev glanced at the tavern she'd just left. "Do they do that a lot? Lie?"

"Nobody can catch them in one, but the way they huff and puff all over town, plenty of us are sure they're compensating for something," he said. "If you ask me, they were low-level goons in the before-times, and were somehow chosen to be the magistrate's right and left hands. The power went to their heads, and they're lording it over the rest of us because they can."

"Hm." Bev reached into her pocket and felt the barley kernels again. She could, of course, ask Gerry, but she didn't quite trust him, especially after what Bernard had said about him.

"Did you happen to see my brother?" Gerry asked.

Bev nodded. "I did. He sends his regards."

"Oh, he does?" The beaked man smiled. "Well, isn't that nice. Maybe there's hope for us yet."

"Are you planning on seeing him soon?" Bev asked. "If the talisman doesn't get returned?"

"Possibly." He winked. "Have a good one, Bev."

~

Bev headed toward Lillie's bakery, Biscuit in

tow. After all, Lillie was the only other person in town Bev trusted, save Merv. The baker's eyes lit up with surprise and indignation when Bev told her what she'd found in the basement of the tavern. She rolled the barley beads around in her hand but couldn't tell if they were real or not.

"Only Percival can do that," she said, handing them back to Bev.

"And he's the only person in town who can do this replication spell?" Bev asked, thinking of that young man with the clipboard who'd been allowing people entry. "There aren't others?"

Lillie shrugged. "I mean, I'm sure there used to be more wizards like him. But down here, he's the only one. Even his apprentice Shamus doesn't really do much with magic. Especially a spell as complex as a replication spell."

Bev nodded. "What all does it entail?"

"I'm not a magicker, but as I understand it, a replication spell is quite the complicated bit of work. Takes a lot of mental acuity and focus, along with the sort of skill that comes from years of practice and knowledge. Even if you had that sort of magic, there's no guarantee you'd be able to accomplish it. We're very lucky that Percival is down here with us."

"How does one get in to see him?" Bev asked.

"Oh, it's really easy. You just queue up, and Shamus lets you back one at a time."

"Shamus?" Bev nodded. "The man with the clipboard? He seemed quite…intense."

"Well, he's got one job, and that's to keep the wizard on schedule or else everyone would be there all day long." She chuckled. "Percival likes to chit-chat, you know. That kind of magic day in and day out is a lot for one person to handle. I think it might've scrambled his brains a bit because he's a little eccentric. But the town would collapse without him, so he keeps at it."

"Stand in line. Seems simple enough." Bev put the barley back in her pocket. "Do you think Percival will be able to tell if something's real or not?"

She nodded. "Oh yes. If it's real barley, then it'll probably disintegrate the moment he tries to replicate it."

"Do you think that'll be enough to prove that someone's getting goods from somewhere else?" Bev asked. "At least enough to clear Merv and me from suspicion?"

"That I can't guarantee," she said. "Nog really likes that tavern, so I hear. I don't think he'd take too kindly to finding out his beer is sourced from Upper Pigsend. Not sure he'd be able to get it anywhere else."

Bev chewed her lip. "I'm not convinced Nog isn't aware of it. Could be some scheme to frame Merv to keep the heat off himself and his tavern-owning friend, you know?"

"Oh, now there's a thought," Lillie said, chopping the nuts with a large knife. "You think he's capable of something like that?"

"I think if the town starts asking how such a thing could've happened, he might want to divert attention away from any passageways he knows about," Bev said. "I guess the first thing to do is make sure this barley isn't magically replicated."

"I'm sure Percival will set you straight." Lillie nodded toward the clock. "But you should get going. The queue is probably out the door already, and I know you've got to get back to the inn."

It was fifteen to eleven. Bev said a prayer for her rising bread dough.

Lillie wasn't kidding about the line. By the time Bev and Biscuit arrived at the Merchant's House, it was almost to the door. People had every sort of object one could imagine, from a bottle of wine to wagons holding planks of wood. There were plenty of things Bev couldn't identify, too—probably magical items that only existed away from Her Majesty's rules.

Bev joined the line in the back, and before long, three more people queued up behind her. The man in front of her had a bucket of nails, and the two ladies behind her had what appeared to be a small dragon that squirmed and twisted in its tiny cage.

Every so often, a puff of smoke would come out, and the shorter of the two ladies would hiss and blow out whatever had caught on fire.

"Pardon," Bev said, curiosity getting the better of her. "What do you need to see the wizard for?"

"We're getting some food replicated for Bertie here," the taller woman said. "He's so particular, and his tastes change every day, it seems. So we've brought several items and whichever he seems to fancy today, we'll ask the wizard to replicate."

"Seems like it's a tough charge to raise a dragon," Bev said. "What kind is he?"

"Oh, he's a horned redtail," the shorter woman said. "Very rare, you know. They make loyal pets, but they can be so particular. Bertie changes his mind like the seasons, and it's all we can do to keep up with his persnicketiness."

Bertie seemed affronted by this insinuation and let out a small stream of flame that caught the shorter woman's tunic on fire.

"Bertie, you bad boy!" She patted her tunic. "You can be an absolute terror, you know that."

The dragon stretched out in its cage and rested his head on its claws, batting his eyes as if he were apologizing.

She cooed and stroked his long neck, shaking her head. "All he has to do is look at me, and all is forgiven," she said with a smile.

"I've never met a dragon," Bev said, looking

closer at the creature. "Unless a dragon shifter counts?"

"Oh, you've met a shifter?"

"Didn't think there were any of those left!"

"What were they like?"

"Well, they were..." How did one explain the grannies? "They liked to eat. Very helpful in rebuilding anything that had been destroyed." She tapped her chin. "There's a young boy back in Pigsend who's also a shifter. They were helping him."

"There's a shifter here in town?" The taller woman put her hand to her mouth.

Bev tutted at herself. By now, she should've remembered where she was and been smarter about the things she said. "No, they're in Upper Pigsend."

They shared a look of surprise which quickly turned into recognition then disdain. "You're the one everyone's talking about."

"The one who's caused all this consternation," the taller lady said. "Stealing our talisman."

"I didn't steal a thing," Bev said. "And who's going around saying that? Officer Nog?"

"Oh, I heard it from Gertrude Kopper, who heard it from Roger Thistle, who heard it from Steward Bigfeather," the shorter lady said. "They said, 'This topsider came down and fought off ten of the magistrate's guards to steal our beloved talisman.' I hear you destroyed half the Merchant's

House, too!"

Bev quirked a brow. In a town this size, Bev hadn't expected to be as "popular" as in Pigsend. But she supposed word traveled fast, even though the truth was a bit slower. "Does it look like the Merchant's House has been destroyed?"

"Well, no." She bristled. "But I'm sure the wizard just cast a spell to fix whatever you broke."

"He's brilliant at that, you know."

"Whatever we need, he makes."

The shorter lady harrumphed once more. "It's amazing the magistrate is letting you walk around, what with your criminal past."

"Supposedly, I have until Officer Bola returns to…" She paused, screwing up her face. "And I *didn't* take your talisman. I was at Steward's that day asking a question about an amulet I was trying to get rid of, because I don't need…" She took a breath, growing weary of having to explain herself. "I hope to have a fruitful conversation with your wizard so we can clear all this up."

The ladies turned their backs on Bev, hemming and hawing to each other and not taking any pains to hide that they were continuing to discuss her. Bev, having been the town pariah during the sinkhole debacle, couldn't believe she'd found herself in the same predicament in yet another town. The urge was strong to turn around and walk back to the inn.

But she couldn't let poor Merv suffer. So she swallowed her anger and remained where she was.

Finally, there were ten people between her and the man with the clipboard. He seemed just as tired and overworked as the day before, asking each person to declare what they wanted magicked and deciding if it was worth the wizard's time. Bev had assumed everyone got to walk through, but at least two people were denied, turning to sulk away with dark looks on their faces.

Bev strained her ears to listen for the reason. It must've been something important, because why would the folks stand in line for hours just to be turned away?

The dragon ladies were next and stepped up to Shamus with smiles on their faces.

"Agatha, Luciene," Shamus said, not looking up. "This is the fifth time this month you've come to see Percival."

"Well, Bertie likes to eat," Agatha said with a smile. "C'mon. We've got a few options for the wizard."

"I'm sorry, but you'll have to wait for your ration like everyone else," Shamus said. "Yours isn't the only dragon who likes to eat. Maybe you can check in with one of the other owners and trade leftover food."

Luciene stomped her foot. "This isn't *fair*, Shamus. We've been standing in line for hours. We *need* more magic than other people."

"And you know the rules." His tone was final. "Next? I—Oh." Shamus looked around the dragon ladies to Bev, and perhaps he knew who she was, because he took a nervous step backward. "What can I do for you?" He cleared his throat. "Looking for a spell you can take to the upside?"

"I had a question for the wizard," Bev said, pulling the barley from her pocket. "Specifically, is this something he's replicated?"

"Nope." Shamus shook his head. "Grains aren't good for magic. Did you bring that from your world?"

Bev looked down at the grains. "I'd like him to take a look at them, just in case. Is that possible? I also have a few questions I need to ask him."

Shamus seemed uncomfortable with the idea. He looked around, almost expecting someone else to pop out of the woodwork and help him, but all he got were the disdainful looks from the two dragon ladies.

"Please," Bev said, lowering her voice, "he doesn't even have to do any magic. I just want to talk with him."

Shamus jutted his thumb at the open door behind him. "Go on, then. But be quick, we have a long line of folks left."

Chapter Twelve

Bev left Biscuit outside and ducked through the red velvet curtains. There were soft candles everywhere—but not on tables. They were floating through the air, circling the room in some preconceived orbit. As one passed Bev, she couldn't help but reach for it—and the candle sped away quickly.

"Yes…?" A voice called weakly. "What is it you've brought for me?"

She scanned the room for the source of the voice and found a withered old man with stringy white hair sitting on a chair. He wore purple robes that hung off his thin frame, and his pointed hat drooped to one side. His face was practically skin and bones, and his eyes were sunken into his skull. But he gave her a weak smile and motioned for her to come closer.

"Goodness me, are you well?" Bev asked.

He barked a laugh, one that made his chest rattle. "Not in some time, but I'm sure I look worse than I feel." He paused. "I don't believe we've met, have we?"

She shook her head. "My name is Bev, I'm—"

"Oh, you're the one causing all the problems, aren't you?" It wasn't said accusatorially, rather a little amusedly.

"Some would say that, yes," Bev said. "I promise you, I had nothing to do with your talisman being stolen. If it even was stolen. I'm not quite sure where we've landed on that. But I do know those magistrate men are keen on bothering my dear friend Merv, so..."

The wizard let out a snore then started himself awake. "Pardon. What were you saying?"

Bev cleared her throat. "I was saying that I'm not responsible for your talisman being taken."

"Oh, of course not. Why do you need a talisman? I'm sure you've plenty of other ways to cast spells." He smiled at her as if he weren't talking complete nonsense.

"I'm not..." Bev cleared her throat. "I have a few questions for you, if you're willing to answer them."

He nodded. "I'm duty-bound to help all who come through my door."

"Er... Right. So about this spell you cast to protect Lower Pigsend," Bev said. "Why is it that I'm able to come and go? Why hasn't the magistrate done anything to protect Merv's tunnel? Or closed it, for that matter? Why—"

Another loud snore then he shook himself awake. "Excuse me, I must've dozed off. What is it you need me to replicate?"

"Ah, not replicate," Bev said, a little concerned for his well-being. "Just asking questions about the talisman's spell and why I'm able to come and go through Merv's tunnel."

"Who is Merv?" He blinked, tilting his head. "And no one can come and go. That's how I designed the spell. It's quite brilliant, you know. One of my best yet, I think."

"I can come and go," she said, waving at him. "Remember? Bev from Pigsend? The one who they say stole the talisman?"

"The talisman's been *stolen?*" He let out a wizened cough. "No, no. That's impossible. Shamus would've told me if that were the case."

Bev let out a breath of frustration. Was this normal for the wizard? Did Shamus have to repeat himself several times? Was—

The wizard snored again then sat upright. "Goodness. I'm so sorry. What was it you wanted me to replicate?"

"Not replicate," Bev tried again. She'd have to be quicker if she wanted to get the answers she was looking for. "My name is Bev. I've been coming and going from Lower Pigsend through a tunnel made by Merv, a moleman. I wanted to know why I was able to. How come the spell doesn't extend to his tunnel?"

"Oh, well." He paused and sounded more coherent than he'd been the entire visit. "Are you a member of the queen's army?"

"Um. No?" Bev shook her head. "I'm an innkeeper."

"Well, then the spell doesn't apply to you." He tilted his head. "It's very specific in nature. It's designed to keep the queen's people out. But in order to do that, I had to balance it by keeping the people of Lower Pigsend in. The rest of the world doesn't apply." He chuckled. "I didn't believe anyone from the topside would want to come down here. It's so dreadfully dark. The only people who want to live here are the ones being hunted by the queen."

"Oh." Bev furrowed her brow. Quite illuminating. "What do you mean, balance?"

"Magic requires balance. If you want it to do something, you have to do something else. A spell as powerful as keeping an entire army out requires a counterbalance of equal proportions." He tilted his head. "Surely, you know that."

"I don't," Bev said. "As I said, I'm just an innkeeper."

He lifted his shoulder.

"And you're sure everyone's…okay with this set up?" Bev asked.

"Of course they are!" He laughed as if she were speaking nonsense. "Everyone here has everything they need. And if they don't, Shamus allows them to come to me, and I can make it for them."

Except those ladies who were denied, and Lillie's flour. And the grain. There were plenty of exceptions Bev could name. She couldn't tell if he was blissfully ignorant of the outside world or willfully so.

"I suppose the magistrate has some say in the spell," Bev said. "Nog and Bola—"

"Who?" His brow furrowed.

"They're officers of the magistrate," Bev said. "They said—"

"No, who are you?" He blinked then shook his head. "I'm sorry, I must've forgotten what we were talking about. It happens from time to time. Now, what was it that you wanted me to replicate?"

"We were discussing the spell that keeps everyone in," Bev said. "And how it seems there are exceptions to it."

"Oh, no exceptions. Everything is as it should be." He beamed. "If there's anything missing, I'll just make more of it. That's what I do, you know."

"And the talisman—"

"The talisman, yes, what a wonderful spell I devised there." He nodded with more gusto than Bev would've thought possible.

Bev sighed. "Do you have any idea why someone would take it?"

"Take it?" He tapped his chin, as if the question were a philosophical one. "Well, the logical answer is they wanted to break the spell keeping them in Lower Pigsend. But it's not out of the question that someone would want the talisman to cast their own spell on it."

"Like what?"

"Oh, I'm sure one could come up with a good answer if one thought about it long enough," he said with a laugh that sounded more like a wheeze. "Still, I can't imagine anyone in Lower Pigsend needing to cast their own spell. I'm quite adept at handling whatever the town needs."

And clearly his body had suffered from it. Even as animated as he'd become, she couldn't ignore the way his breath rattled in his chest, the wispy nature of his hair, the far-off look in his eye.

"If we don't find the talisman, are you going to be able to cast another spell?" Bev asked. "To keep the protections the same?"

"I believe that…"

Bev leaned in. "You believe…?"

"I believe in the stars and the wind and the

rain." His pale eyes swept up, and his gaze danced along the ceiling as the candles moved in the other direction. "I believe in the water in the ground. And the movement of the magic." He stopped abruptly, his gaze falling back to Bev. "I'm sorry, you had something for me to replicate?"

Shamus was probably chomping at the bit, getting ready to barge in to tell her to leave, so instead of trying to rehash what she'd already learned, she just asked the last question she had. "Are these barley pearls magically replicated?"

"Oh, no, no." He shook his head. "The magic doesn't do well with the grains." He weakly lifted his hand to poke at them in her outstretched palm. Bev thought his fingers might break off. "No, these are fresh. Wherever did you get them?"

"From a tavern here in town," Bev said. "I think there might be another tunnel to the upside. One that's being used to bring in goods like this barley."

"That's impossible," he said with a chuckle. "The spell is quite complete. No one in or out."

"Except me," Bev said. "And Merv. And the magistrate's men—"

"I'm sorry, who?" He blinked again. "Pardon. I must've dozed off for a second. Do you have something for me to replicate?"

Bev sat back, sympathy filling her mind for this poor soul. She obviously didn't know anything about magic, but the toll it was taking on the wizard was more than just physical.

"Percival," Bev said quietly, pocketing the barley kernels again, "are you in this state because the talisman was stolen? Forgetting trains of thought? Forgetting people who were just speaking with you?"

Another laugh rattled his chest. "I'm not young by any stretch, but a wizard is not meant to keep an entire town fed and clothed, especially not by magical means."

"You could stop," Bev said. "It looks to be taking all of you with it."

"And I'm sure it will, some day. But when I go, there will be no one left to keep this place from falling into ruin. The people who've found safe haven here will have to return to the upper world once more. And that will be a sad day indeed." He let out a weary sigh. "I don't think any of us planned to be down here so long. But here we are, and here I am."

The urge was strong to take his hand, but Bev kept her distance. "I appreciate your time. Thank you for your help."

"Time. Time is moving slowly, and yet very, very quickly. The world turns, but not for us." His eyes had taken on that glassy expression again. "I'm sorry. I must've lost myself for a moment. You said you had something for me to replicate?"

~

Bev walked out through the front door, finding Biscuit waiting for her with a wagging tail. She patted him on the head absentmindedly, her attention on the line of people clutching their wares, eagerly waiting to be seen. Before Bev had even gotten out, the next person bustled past her carrying a single sprig of something that left a trail of glowing dust on the ground, which Biscuit found very interesting. They, certainly, didn't seem to care that the man on the other side was barely clinging to sanity—perhaps even life. Would they throw down their wares, demand a spell, then leave before realizing that the man was giving his life for them?

He came out a moment later, the single sprig turned into a bushel. And the next person hurried inside.

Did *anyone* speak with him at all, or was it just business as usual? Go in, cast the spell, come out. What a horrible life.

Bev caught Shamus eyeing her suspiciously, and she balled up her fists as she walked up to him. "Are you aware of what all these spells are doing to him?"

"If you have questions for me, go to the back of the line," he said, purposefully looking at his clipboard as he waved the next person past.

"No, I think I can ask you right here," Bev said. "That poor man can barely hold a conversation. How do you expect him to—"

"*If* you have *questions*," Shamus said through

gritted teeth, "*you* can go to the back of the line and wait. There's no need to cause a scene in front of these people."

"But—"

"And if you don't move in the next few minutes, I shall ring Officer Nog to have you arrested for disturbing the peace."

Bev was about to argue more, but the clock on the wall began chiming. *Dong - dong - dong*

Three.

"It can't be three o'clock in the afternoon," Bev gasped, her heart sinking into her stomach. Had she really lost track of time?

Her bread was going to be a *mess*.

"This conversation isn't over," Bev said, pointing an accusatory finger at Shamus before turning to hightail it back to Merv's tunnel.

~

Bev was out of breath by the time she reached Merv's home, and even Biscuit, who was indefatigable, was breathing hard. The moleman was awake, knitting yet another blanket, and jumped upright when Bev and Biscuit walked through his door without knocking.

"Bev, goodness me! You scared me half to death."

"So sorry, Merv," she said, continuing through without breaking her pace. "Got to get back to the inn. The day got away from me."

"But I—"

"Be back tomorrow!"

The journey back to the inn seemed the longest yet. Bev winced as she passed the clock; it was closer to four than three. By now, her bread should've been on its second proofing, perhaps even getting ready for the oven. Dinner should've been bubbling away, but she hadn't even *ordered* her meat yet. Wim McKee would be turning in his grave if he knew how poorly she'd managed the day.

She burst into the Weary Dragon, clutching her chest and babbling apologies. But there wasn't anyone waiting for her. No one in the chair, no one standing by the front desk. The fire, which had been roaring this morning, had gone out, and the whole room held a chill.

"Well." Bev put her hand to her head, wiping away the sweat and feeling more than a little disappointed as Biscuit went to lap water from his bowl in the kitchen. "Let's see what we have to work with."

Her bread dough, as feared, was an absolute mess. She'd half a mind to throw it out, but if Etheldra didn't get her rosemary bread, Bev would hear about it. So she did her best to shape and stick them in the baskets then put them in the warmest spot in the kitchen and said a prayer.

Another glance at the clock—no time to go to the butchers. Well, she did have barley on the brain, so barley soup it would have to be.

Dinner came together at the last minute, including the bread, which was such a poor effort Bev was embarrassed to put it out. But the absence of bread was traditionally met with more complaining, so Bev hoped her performance would be enough to satisfy.

Unfortunately, her three regulars had dined with her enough to tell the difference.

"Well, this is…certainly something," Etheldra said, eyeing the spread with more than a little distaste. "Barley soup? Are things that lean lately?"

"No, just thought I'd mix it up for a change," Bev said.

"You certainly did that."

"Is everything all right, Bev?" Earl asked. "I've been by three times this week, and you haven't been at your post. Got worried until I popped in to see Allen, and he said you were busy but all right."

"Oh…" Bev cleared her throat. "I've been elsewhere. Helping a friend."

"And does this *friend* know you're putting your own livelihood at risk to help them?" Etheldra asked, closely inspecting the rosemary bread.

"I'm not—"

"I've had no fewer than five travelers pass through my tea shop today, all of them waiting for an hour for the absent innkeeper to return," Etheldra said.

Five? Bev winced. That was certainly a huge hit.

"Now I don't know about you," Etheldra continued, "but that's a concerning pattern for any business owner. And now you serve us this *barley* soup?"

"Etheldra—" Bardoff began.

But the teashop owner wasn't to be deterred. "If you keep doing shoddy work like this, you might lose your three best customers."

"No, she won't, Etheldra. Not after all Bev's done for this town," Earl said with a warning glance. "And I'm sure whatever Bev's up to is worth the time she's spending away from the inn." He gave her a sideways glance. "Right?"

"I'm hoping to have it all wrapped up tomorrow," Bev said with a thin smile.

She wasn't anywhere near to figuring it out, but she had to say something to get the three scrutinizing glances off her.

Chapter Thirteen

As she cleaned up after dinner, Bev couldn't help but agree with Etheldra. It was hard to be in two places at once, let alone two places that were so far apart. It wasn't like when mischief happened in Upper Pigsend, and Bev could spend most of her time at the inn and still tend to customers. Not that she was in dire straits financially, but too many days turning away paying customers was terrible for business. The local diners paid monthly, but the amount of food Bev made always cost more than they paid, as she always anticipated a guest or two joining them. She was going to have to dip into the stash of gold coins she kept under the floorboard if she didn't figure out a way to rent rooms to guests while she wasn't here. Not to mention magically make dinner appear.

"It's a good thing Merv is such a dear friend," Bev said as she wiped down the tables in the front room.

But perhaps her motivation had shifted, especially after speaking with Percival. She couldn't believe the people of the town hadn't noticed his current state, yet they continued to queue up, seeming not to care at all about how their requests affected him.

"Percival will fix it!" Gerry had said, as if it were a foregone conclusion. Did he know Percival could barely carry on a conversation?

But who Bev could bring this to in Lower Pigsend was another matter. Nog seemed more concerned with lording over the townsfolk, destroying perfectly good cake and the like. Bev doubted he was even *looking* for the missing talisman. And Shamus, too, stood in front of the queue, shuffling people inside. When was the last time he'd spoken to his master?

"And I thought we had problems up here," Bev said to Biscuit.

Biscuit, unsurprisingly, didn't respond.

She finished sweeping the front room and headed into the kitchen to clean in there. The leftover bread dough sat on the counter, ready to be put to bed until morning. But Bev watched it for a moment, chewing her lip. Lillie had said it was possible to proof it overnight, especially if Bev had a cold place like a root cellar. She did have that, and the nights weren't yet so warm.

"Well, maybe we give it a go," Bev said. "Couldn't be worse than tonight's performance, I'd say."

She gathered her ingredients—flour, water, barm, salt, rosemary. She'd used the last of what she had in the canister she kept in the kitchen, and said a small prayer there was more in the root cellar. Typically, she wouldn't combine her ingredients until the morning, and doing it so soon seemed somewhat wrong, especially since she wasn't planning on baking until tomorrow afternoon at the usual time.

But as she combined everything in a bowl, she found herself genuinely curious what would happen. Obviously, experimenting for the Harvest Festival needed to take a backseat, but if she could save herself the trouble of needing to make bread in the morning, it was worth a try.

The mixture sat for about half an hour while Bev cleaned the rest of the kitchen, then she kneaded it a few times until it came together in a ball and plopped it into one of her large kitchen bowls. Covering it with a tea towel, she carried it outside, much to the curiosity of Biscuit—and even Sin, who brayed at her from the stables.

"Yes, yes, it's strange. But we're experimenting," Bev said to her animals.

She headed to her root cellar, only stopping to grab her glowing stick so she could see what she was doing. She tucked the bread bowl near her potatoes in a cool spot then turned to assess the rest of her cellar. Three bags identical to the one she'd found at the tavern sat against the wall, bearing Sonny's emblem. The flour one was almost empty, but there was enough for one batch in the morning, thankfully. Everything else seemed low, too—potatoes, carrots, parsnips. She was in dire need of a visit to the farmers' market tomorrow.

"Maybe I can pick some up in Lower Pigsend," Bev said half-jokingly to Biscuit.

But she couldn't really find the humor in it.

She reached into her pocket to examine the barley pearls from Lower Pigsend. They certainly looked the same as the ones she'd put into the soup this evening. Tasted the same, too.

"Well, we do need to visit Sonny in the morning to get some more flour. Might as well ask him who he's selling barley to," Bev said, returning to the kitchen to get her canister. She dumped the remaining flour from the larger bag into the smaller vessel. It would barely be enough to do another loaf in the morning, but she could manage, if she had to. And Sonny would be open around nine. If worse came to worst on the overnight proof, she'd still have time to get everything together.

She returned to the kitchen with the full canister of flour and finished tidying up. She was quite tired, and when she thought about all the questions left unanswered in Lower Pigsend, it felt more like exhaustion. Wearily, she climbed the stairs to her bedroom, Biscuit following, and changed into her pajamas before climbing into bed.

And this time, she fell asleep before her head hit the pillow.

For the fourth day in a row, Bev rose early, the sting of Etheldra's words hovering over everything she did. Once again, she blessed the silver lining of not having any guests and no guest laundry to tend to. But, of course, the rest of her day lay before her as it always did.

Before starting on her morning bread, she popped down to the root cellar to check on her overnight proof. Holding her breath in anticipation, she pulled back the tea towel to reveal…

Well, it wasn't exactly proofed, but it wasn't a mess, either.

She poked the top of it, wondering if she should go ahead and shape it or let it rise some more. If she left it in here, the chill would keep it from growing too much, but would she be back in time to pull it out so it could rise completely? Hard to say.

In the end, she opted to leave it. Underproofed

was somewhat better than overproofed, and she would keep a better eye on the clock today. Just to be on the safe side, she made another loaf to process the usual way, using up the rest of the flour she'd put in her canister the night before. At least visiting the miller wouldn't take her too far out of town— and she might be able to get a few answers to her questions about the barley, too.

She was just putting on her traveling cloak when the front door opened. Allen walked in with a basket of sweets, accompanied by Vicky's younger brother Grant, PJ Norris, who was still sporting the talisman that kept him from transforming into a giant dragon, and Valta Climber, the younger sister of the blacksmith's apprentice.

"Morning, Bev!" Allen announced chipperly. "How's it going?"

"What's all this?" Bev asked. "I'm afraid there aren't any guests this morning. Turns out when you aren't here to man the front desk, they move on."

"Ah, yeah. I heard about that." He rested his hands on Grant and PJ's shoulders. "And I think I have a solution to your problem." He paused. "Well, not the big one, but the problem of your inn. These three *industrious* young folks are in need of jobs. They can certainly help run the inn while you're gone."

Based on the kids' expressions, they'd much rather be in bed. "Really?" Bev asked.

"They're happy to do it, aren't you?" Allen said, squeezing their shoulders. "Especially PJ. It was his idea, after all."

The dragon shifter ducked his head and nodded. "After what you did for me, it's the least we can do."

She tilted her head at him. "I didn't do much, PJ. The grannies really—"

"You did plenty," he said. "Right, guys?"

Valta and Grant nodded.

"Well, I'd be grateful for the help, but I can't pay you much," Bev said with a half-lift of her shoulder. "Maybe half a silver each per day?"

Their faces perked up. "Half a silver to just sit here and watch the inn?" Valta asked.

"Well, I might have you do a bit around the place, too. Tend to the mule, tidy the laundry, that sort of thing," Bev said, thinking more about it. "One of you can sit at the counter. I'll show you how to sign people in and which keys go to which rooms. Another one of you can join me in the kitchen. There are still some dishes to scrub, and I can show you what to look for when the bread is ready to be shaped." She paused, giving Allen a grateful smile. "Yes, I think this will do just fine. Thank you."

"Don't mention it," he said, walking to the door before pausing. "And I'll be sure to keep an eye on them while you're gone."

~

Bev led the three kids into the kitchen, noticing all the things she'd put off in her haste to get out the door and feeling doubly grateful someone would be here to tackle them while she was gone.

"I'd start with these," she said, pointing to the dishes she'd only halfway finished. "Scrub them clean and get them ready for dinner."

"You don't clean them at night?" Grant asked, peering into the sink with a frown on his face. PJ gave him a dirty look, and he cleared his throat. "I mean, sure. Happy to help."

Bev continued, "Around ten, head over to the butcher shop to order two pounds of meat. If you three are planning on staying for dinner, make it four, and if anyone happens to come by looking for a room, add half a pound per person."

"What kind of meat?" PJ asked.

"Your choice, I suppose. Depending on what the butchers have." Bev turned to point at the back door. "They should have it ready around noon, at which point you can head to the root cellar and find some potatoes and other vegetables. Just give them a rough chop and toss them into that pan." She pointed to the one in the sink. "Make sure it's all cooking before two." She stopped. "You do know how to operate the oven, right?"

"PJ can just breathe some fire into it," Grant said with a wry grin.

"Har har." PJ glared at him. "Yeah, I think we

can figure out the oven."

Bev forced a smile. "If you have trouble, Allen should be able to help."

Bev turned to the dough proofing in the bowl. Her instinct was to tell them to leave her precious bread alone, but…that had been an unmitigated disaster the day before. It would have to be shaped and put into the baskets by midday, and she couldn't be sure she'd be around to do it.

"As far as the bread." She pulled today's batch from its spot and lifted the tea towel to show the kids. "You see the size of it now, and how it's dense?" She poked it, and they nodded. "In a few hours, it's going to double in size. Basically be to the top of this bowl, yeah?"

"All by itself?" PJ asked, looking at the bowl.

"As long as it stays in this warm spot. After it doubles, you'll want to shape it and let it rise again." Bev replaced the towel. "And the other batch…" She tapped her finger to her chin, thinking. "You know, I was going to let it sit in its bowl for longer, but I can show you how to shape them."

She went to the cellar to retrieve her bowl of bread, bringing it to the kitchen table as the three kids and Allen gathered around. She dumped the dough onto her floured table, talking them through her next steps.

"So you take a knife and cut it into three equal-sized pieces," Bev said, slicing the dough into thirds.

"Then, you'll want to shape it like this."

She tugged the edges of one of the dough sections out until it was a flat rectangle. Then she folded the two long ends over on themselves, and began rolling from the bottom, pulling the dough slightly toward her.

"You try." Bev nodded to the other two dough sections.

PJ took one, and Valta took the other, with Grant standing back and watching with a scowl on his face. Bev guided them through it, resisting the urge to step in and do it for them.

"You'll want to do that same treatment to the batch over by the oven around one o'clock today," Bev said. "Assuming I'm not back yet…"

"Where have you been going?" PJ asked. "Allen didn't say."

Bev had been erring on the side of not telling anyone about Lower Pigsend, just in case someone from the queen's service showed up, but for PJ, she'd make an exception. There was a not-small chance the boy might be in need of a place to hide his magical abilities. Not that she wanted him transforming into a dragon down there, but with the talisman around his neck, there shouldn't be any danger of that.

"Are you kids familiar with Lower Pigsend?" Bev asked.

They shook their heads.

"Well, it's an underground town. Since the war, it's where all the magical refugees have found safe haven. If you remember Merv the moleman—"

"Oh, yeah, I remember seeing him," PJ said. "During the sinkhole thing, right?"

Bev nodded. "Very recently, the talisman that protects the town went missing. The guards believe Merv…" She paused. "Well, they don't believe he took it, but they're accusing him of basically leaving the door open. I'm trying to prove there's another way in and out, so they'll leave him alone."

"You aren't looking for the talisman itself?" PJ asked. "Seems like if you found that, all would be fixed, right?"

She nodded. "It would, but it's a big town, and I wouldn't know where to begin. Supposedly, there's a guard looking for it, but he seems to change his story every time I see him." She shook her head, saving them the details. "In any case, I need to visit the miller today to get some more flour, and also to ask him some questions."

"The miller?" PJ asked. "What would he know about Lower Pigsend?"

"I suppose that's what I'm going to find out," Bev said. "Was just about to get the mule hooked up to the wagon to go when you three got here."

"I can do that," PJ said. "And I can go with you, and bring her back, too. That way you can head straight back to Lower Pigsend from there."

Bev smiled. He was awfully helpful, this young lad. "Well, then that's settled. Grant and Valta, you can stay here and get started on the kitchen chores, and PJ will come with me."

The other teens made a face like they'd much rather go with Bev, but PJ was already out the door, headed to Sin's barn.

"Are you sure you two will be all right?" Bev asked Grant as he slowly plodded to the sink.

"It's an inn." He shrugged, picking up a scrubber. "How hard can it be?"

Chapter Fourteen

While PJ got Sin hooked up to the wagon, Bev gave Valta a quick primer on which keys went to which rooms, and what she should say to the guests as they arrived.

"It's one gold for a night, which includes dinner," Bev said. "Which is why...erm...it's important that we have dinner. So—"

"So yeah, go to the butchers," Valta said. "Anything else?"

Bev wanted to say something about Valta's sneer, or the way she slumped into the front chair, but beggars couldn't be choosers. At least there'd be someone at the inn, and an attempt at dinner. Until Bev figured out this mess in Lower Pigsend, that was as good as she could hope for.

With the other two teenagers sorted, Bev and Biscuit walked out back. Bev retrieved her empty flour bag and tossed it into the back of the wagon, before lifting Biscuit to sit next to it and climbing in herself.

"Bringing the dog?" PJ asked, sitting in the driver's seat.

"He's quite handy," Bev said as Biscuit sniffed around the bottom of the wagon. "He can sniff out magic. I'm going to turn him loose around Sonny's mill and maybe he'll find a trail to Lower Pigsend."

PJ eyed Biscuit as he caught a nose full of flour from underneath the wagon seat and sneezed.

"Is that how he found me? He sniffed out my magic?" he asked quietly as he snapped the reins and goaded Sin forward. "When I was about to…"

"Yes, and how he found the grannies and brought them to you in the nick of time," Bev said. "Lucky, lucky. All of us."

"I keep waiting for Flanigan to come back," PJ said, casting a wary eye around the town as Sin clopped on the street toward the east. "Can't believe he was fooled. Surely, he's got to suspect the grannies."

Valta and Grant, in a fit of genius, had used a combination of a sky lantern and a bag full of cinnamon to make a convincing dragon, one that had led Flanigan and his band of soldiers out of

Pigsend and allowed PJ and the grannies to flee to safety.

"He might've, but a man like Flanigan probably has a thousand leads to follow," Bev said. "He even said *I* was a person of interest."

"You?" PJ chuckled. "For what? Making too much bread?"

Bev didn't answer, not wanting to give the local rumor mill any more than it already had.

"Did the grannies give you any other instructions? What to do if you felt like transforming again?" Bev asked, as they passed through the town square. "Did they say if they'd be back?"

"No, and no." He pulled the talisman out from under his shirt. "They said as long as I wear this, I shouldn't have any more urges to transform. And I haven't, either." He tucked it back against his chest. "They told me that while the queen's in charge, the only thing for me to do is lie low, keep the amulet on, and stay out of trouble."

"And you've done a good job of it," Bev said with a nod.

"One full transformation was enough for me, thank you. Bad enough I was breaking buildings all over town. My parents still can't believe it...and they're grateful no one else in town knows what really happened either." He cast her a sideways look. "Grateful to you, Bev, for all you did for me. If it weren't for you..." He shivered. "I don't even want to think about it."

"And your friends?"

"Eh, they need something to do," he said, sounding much older than his years would suggest. "Grant's moping around because his sister is getting married, and Valta's been whining about her parents pulling her from school to work the farm." He shook his head. "They're both in need of direction, and perhaps they'll be inspired by working at the inn."

"Goodness, PJ, you sound like Bardoff," Bev said.

He blushed, thumbing the reins.

"You did come at the right time, I will say. I was starting to worry about how all this was affecting the inn."

"You must really love this moleman guy to go through all this trouble," PJ said.

"Well, he's been a huge help over the past few months. And it's unfair for him to take the blame for something that clearly wasn't his fault." Bev made a face. "Especially since those charged with protecting the town seem keen on doing anything *but* protecting it. I get the feeling that I'm the only one interested in finding out the truth."

They left the main part of town and headed down the road that led to the miller's. Trent Scrawl was once again out in his fields, inspecting the vines for signs of wear and presumably keeping them safe from his nemesis Herman Monday. Bev waved at him, but he just scowled at her.

"Do you really think Sonny's mixed up in something bad?" PJ asked. "He seems nice enough whenever we have to come out and reshoe his horse. He's always busy, too. Lots of folks coming and going."

"He's a lovely person," Bev said. "I don't think he has any idea the person buying his barley is effectively smuggling it into the town. If anything, I'm hoping he can give me a name or a description or *something* I can use to pinpoint who it is."

"And you're the only one who can investigate this?" PJ asked. "They don't have their own version of Sheriff Rustin down there?"

"I think their version of Rustin is the one causing the problems," Bev said, thinking of Nog in Lonny's bar. "Which is part of the mystery I'm trying to unravel. Who knows why they're keen on keeping it a secret from the rest of the town? There's something larger afoot, some piece I'm missing that might reveal everything."

"So this is what you do, then? Just find a mystery and solve it?" PJ asked.

"I'd like to think my job is keeping the Weary Dragon up, but…lately it seems you're correct."

Sin pulled the wagon right up to the front door of the mill, having made this trek many times in her long life. The large wheel was turning steadily, aided by the water in Pigsend Creek. As often as Bev had come here, she was filled with trepidation. Sonny was, as she'd told PJ, a lovely person, and she'd never had a cross word from him. But whenever she had these sorts of confrontations, even the nicest person grew testy with her. Obviously, Bev needed to maintain a good relationship with him, lest she lose her supply of flour for her rosemary bread.

She slipped off the wagon bench and put Biscuit on the ground, kneeling to his level as she scratched his head.

"Listen closely," Bev said. "I want you to sniff around and see what you can find, okay? If you pick up on a thread of magic, come back and get me, and we'll follow it together."

He looked up at her, and Bev could've sworn he nodded.

"Keep on task," she said, patting him on the head. "Don't go hunting down Sonny's breakfast or anything like that."

He let his tongue fall out in a smile as he put his nose to the ground and headed west.

"So…you can talk to him, too?" PJ asked, coming up beside her.

"I told you, he's a special kind of dog," Bev said, watching him closely inspect a bush. Just as she thought he might've found something, he lifted his leg to urinate. "For the most part." She grabbed the empty flour bag and walked inside.

The sound of the mill grinding the wheat into flour echoed loudly. Sonny, an older man with a bald head and a stout frame, stood near the large stone, watching it work carefully, but smiled when he saw Bev.

"Well, hey there, Bev!" He waved, blissfully oblivious of Bev's trepidation. "Haven't seen you in a spell. And young Pip Junior! What are you doing here?"

"He's helping me out at the inn today," Bev said.

"Oh?" Sonny turned to the boy. "Your parents let you out of the family business for a bit?"

"He's working off a bit of mischief he and his friends got into," Bev said, thinking quickly. It wasn't the most unbelievable thing, as the trio *had* gotten into mischief at the inn a few weeks ago. "In any case, he's here to help me get a new bag of flour."

"Aren't you in luck? Just finished a batch a few minutes ago." He walked to the wall where ten bags of flour sat. "Take your pick!"

"Just the one," Bev said, handing the miller the empty bag. "PJ, would you be a dear and load that up onto the wagon for me?"

"You got it." He hoisted the nearest bag over his shoulder and disappeared through the door.

"What kind of trouble did he get into?" Sonny

asked.

"Threw some flour with his friends," Bev said. "All very innocent, but Bardoff was keen they learn a lesson." She paused. "Hey, Sonny, how well do you keep track of your bags?"

"What do you mean?"

"I mean, obviously, I bring mine back to exchange," she said. "Does everyone?"

"For the most part," he said. "Haven't had to buy new ones in an age. Most of my customers are pretty keen on getting that half-a-silver discount." He smiled as he turned to her. "Why?"

"I just…thought I saw one in an unusual place," Bev said. "Who all do you sell to?"

He tilted his head in confusion. "What d'ya mean?"

"I mean, obviously you sell to me, to Allen Mackey. Who else?" Bev asked.

"Well, anyone else who comes by, I guess." He scratched the back of his neck. "Not sure what you're asking."

"How often do you sell to someone who isn't from Pigsend?" Bev asked, trying her best to dance around the question without fully coming out with it. "Or someone you've never seen around town before?"

He stared at her like she had two heads. "I mean, people come from all over. Not really another mill until you reach Middleburg."

"But does anyone else buy barley from you? I mean, other than me."

"Oh yeah, people buy it for stews and soups and whatnot."

"Anyone named Lonny?" Bev asked.

He scratched his head. "No. Nobody by that name, I don't think. But you never know. People come from all over, and sometimes I don't catch their name. Why do you ask?"

"I guess I was just wondering if you could tell if this barley came from your mill or not," Bev said, reaching into her pocket.

He picked up one and inspected it. "I mean, it looks like barley to me. Not really any way to put my stamp on a single pearl like that, you know?" He chuckled and handed it back to her. "What in the world's gotten into you, Bev? What's with all the questions, eh?" He paused, his eyes lighting up. "Do you have some sort of new mystery in town you're trying to figure out? Someone illegally brewing beer?"

"You could say that." It was, perhaps, a mistake to believe Sonny would give her a name she recognized. "Never mind. Ignore me." She handed over a gold coin. "Thanks for the flour. Appreciate it."

"Are you sure you're all right, Bev?" Sonny asked.

"Just..." She sighed as she headed toward the

door. "If you think of anyone who might strike you as strange, even halfway interesting, catch their name and keep it for me, will you?"

He nodded. "Sure will."

~

"Something tells me that didn't go well," PJ said, sitting atop the wagon with the bag of flour in the back.

"No. No it didn't," Bev said with a sigh. "And now I've got to head down to Lower Pigsend without a clue what to do next." She clutched the kernels again. "As much as I hate to admit it, I feel like I might be out of my depth here."

Biscuit reappeared by her legs and sat, looking up at her with something of a disappointed expression.

"You were unsuccessful, too?" she asked the laelaps.

He sniffed loudly.

"Well, back to the depths I go, I suppose," Bev said. "PJ, can you take that flour to the inn and get Sin in her stable? Might be a good day to let her out in the pen, too. The sun feels nice."

"Is there anything else I can do?" PJ asked.

Bev glanced at the countryside before remembering what day it was. If she did have help for the day, no use in not sending them on *all* the errands. "Actually, there is. In my bedroom, you'll find a loose floorboard with some gold coins. Take one and Sin and the wagon to the Pigsend Farmers' Market. Do you know where that is?"

"I'm sure I can find it."

"I don't know what they've got, but perhaps they have something that would be good with dinner," Bev said. "Definitely potatoes, carrots, that sort of thing. Find a farmer named Alice and tell her you're there to buy for me. I'm sure she'll set you straight."

"Will do." He snapped the reins, and he was on his way.

Bev knelt to Biscuit's level and scratched him behind the ears. "Really? No magical trail? Not even a hint of magic?"

Another sniff.

"They must be hiding their tracks well." She rose as her wagon disappeared over a hill. "As much as I'd like you to come with me to Lower Pigsend, I feel you might be better suited to keeping an eye on the kids at the inn for me. Goodness knows we can't weather too many more disastrous afternoons."

He unfurled his tongue in a smile.

"Yes, yes. If I remember, I'll bring you back something from Lillie's bakery," she said with a chuckle. "Now run along, you little pig."

Biscuit popped upright and trotted along the tracks Bev's wagon had made. She waited until the white tip of his tail disappeared over the hump in the road before turning on her heel and walking in the direction of Merv's tunnel.

"Oh, good, you're still here!" Sonny walked out from the mill. "I was just thinking about what you asked me. There *is* a curious-looking gentleman who comes every few weeks to pick up a bag of barley. Nothing else. No oats, no flour, just the barley."

"Really?" Bev turned to him. "What's his name?"

"Gosh." He rubbed his head. "I want to say Walt? Maybe William?"

That name didn't ring a bell. "He doesn't look…erm…" How to describe him? "Green?"

"Green? Goodness, no. Just a normal man. Maybe twenty-five or thirty. Dark hair, pale skin. All business, though. Don't see where he comes from or where he goes." He tilted his head. "Does that help you at all?"

"Certainly gives me a little to go on." It could've been anyone in Lower Pigsend or anyone from the countryside. "If you see him again, would you be a dear and let me know?"

"I sure will." He brightened. "Boy, it sure is nice to be included in one of these Bev mysteries! I hear about them all the time from Allen. You're quite the clever innkeeper."

The clock chimed from the town in the distance. Ten o'clock. The day was getting away from her.

"Thank you, Sonny. If you think of anything else, please let me know."

Chapter Fifteen

Bev walked the length of Merv's tunnel, wishing her chat with Sonny had been more fruitful. She hadn't gotten a good look at the man who'd bought the tanddaes from Bathilda, so she hadn't a clue if he was the same man Sonny had described. She certainly didn't have a name to check, and Sonny hadn't sounded confident in his memory, either. All in all, another dead end.

Still, Bev trudged dutifully toward Merv's house, intent on making the best of her help back at the inn. Most of the morning had been spent at Sonny's and getting the kids set with managing things, but she still had a few hours to spend in Lower Pigsend. What, exactly, she was going to do there remained something of a mystery, but she'd come up with something.

Merv seemed to have heard her coming, because he opened the door before she could even knock.

"Tell me you've got good news," Merv said as he ushered Bev inside his house, a handkerchief the size of a tablecloth in his hand as he blew his nose. "I need some this morning."

"What happened?" Bev had never seen Merv cry before. "What's going on?"

"Officer Nog stopped by again this morning," he said, dabbing his dark eyes with it. "Says he's *testing* the spell just outside my door. But I think he's just keen on harassing me."

"I have a feeling he does that," Bev said with narrowed eyes. "What did he say about the spell?"

"Says it's in its last days," he said. "That if the talisman's not returned to its spot soon, the whole town's going to be in danger, and it's all my fault."

"And did he say he thinks the talisman is still in Lower Pigsend?" Bev asked. "Because his story seems to change every time I speak with him."

Merv let out a forlorn sigh. "I'm not sure, to be honest. All I know is he was checking the barrier then came back in and berated me for my carelessness, and how I was going to be responsible for the downfall of thousands of souls." He blew his nose. "I'm beside myself with worry—and running out of yarn!"

There were no fewer than five new blankets folded on the table since the day before. Bev swallowed her anger at Nog for getting Merv in a tizzy, when it was plain as day that he had his own unsanctioned tunnel.

"Has Lillie been by already?" Bev asked, nodding to the full box of cookies on the table.

"She came over to check on me again, sweet thing," he said. "Brought me a fresh batch of cookies, but I'm still working through those she made me yesterday. They pack a punch, for sure. She promises today's cookies aren't quite as potent, but you know, I can't be falling asleep at the drop of a hat. Not when Nog's sniffing around, accusing me of…well, you know."

"I saw him yesterday," Bev said. "In a tavern owned by a man named Lonny. Are you familiar?"

Merv sat in his chair and started working on yet another blanket. "Somewhat. I'm not a big ale drinker."

"Well, I went there to see about his beer," Bev said. "Nog was there, and when I asked him how they managed to brew beer without barley, he told me it was magically replicated. But Biscuit and I managed to sneak into his basement, and we found bags of barley with the markings of the Pigsend miller."

"Goodness!" Merv gasped. "And right under Nog's nose?"

"I can't square whether he knows or not," Bev said. "So to be sure, I went to check with the wizard, and…Merv, have you *seen* Percival? He's nothing but skin and bones and barely able to hold a conversation." She paused. "I asked him why the tunnel allowed you and me to come and go to Lower Pigsend, and *he* said it was because he hadn't accounted for us in his spell. Said it was balanced, that he was able to keep the queen's people out by keeping the people of Lower Pigsend in. But he hadn't included the innocent folk not affiliated with the queen."

Merv nodded thoughtfully. "I'm not as well-versed in magic as Percival, but that does make sense."

"Now, that doesn't account for how Nog and Bola were able to get to the Weary Dragon, or how the tanddaes got from Bathilda's to the Merchant's House, so I'm not sure that's the whole picture," Bev said with a huff. "But every time I tried to get a straight answer out of the wizard, his eyes went fuzzy and he'd start talking nonsense. Poor man has one foot in the grave from all the magic they're asking of him." She shook her head. "It was sad, Merv. And I worry that Shamus fellow is letting it go on without a care in the world."

"Oh, now, Shamus is a good man," Merv said. "He's been Percival's faithful assistant all these years. Why would he do anything to harm his master?"

Bev didn't know, but something about the way he'd shooed her off when she was asking questions made her uneasy.

"Well, at the end of it, Percival did confirm that the barley wasn't magically replicated, which means *someone's* not telling the truth," Bev said with a sigh. "But I have a feeling if I confront Nog about it, he'll give me some kind of excuse why this particular barley is allowed. He's friends with the barkeep where I found this stuff. Maybe he's been using the same tunnel as Bathilda's buyer." She paused. "Which, by the way, I stopped by Sonny's before coming here, and he gave me a name. William or Walt. Ring a bell?"

Merv shook his head. "There are so many people in Lower Pigsend. Lillie may have heard of someone with that name."

"I may stop by there," Bev said. "But honestly, I haven't a clue what to do about Officer Nog. He doesn't want to play by the rules on a good day. Is there anyone who can rein him in? Shamus, perhaps?"

"I would take your concerns to the magistrate," Merv said. "That's Nog's boss, after all."

"Where do I find him?" Bev asked.

"In the Merchant's House, I believe. But I've never had reason to seek him out."

"No one has, it sounds like," Bev said. "Lillie hasn't either."

"I bet you Steward has." Merv opened the new box of cookies and offered one to Bev. She shook her head and he plucked one from the box and popped it into his mouth. "He's always doing something for Nog and Bola, so he must've met with the magistrate once or twice. I'm sure he could..."

His words slurred off as his whole snout drooped forward.

"Guess she was still a little heavy-handed with that relaxing potion," Bev said with a sigh as she picked up one of Merv's blankets and covered him with it. "Rest up, Merv. I suppose I've got to visit Steward again."

~

It was a good thing Bev had a decent memory (well, these days) because she was able to find her way to Steward's shop without much trouble. As she turned this way and that, she overheard more anxious conversations from the townsfolk, many of whom were discussing what they'd do when the magic ran out in a few days. More than one said they were already packing their belongings to make a hasty exit, but none of them knew what to expect in the coming days. Bev couldn't help but feel sorry for them and agitated on their behalf that their so-called guards weren't doing more to help.

She found Steward's shop and let herself inside. She was quite sure there were more books than before, stacked in the same haphazard piles that seemed almost ready to topple over. How the scribe was able to find anything was nothing short of a miracle.

"Steward?" Bev called. "Are you here?"

There was a small chirp from somewhere far away, followed by the sound of pages rippling in the breeze. A shadow descended from above—Bev blinked, having not looked that way before. There were more books crammed into nooks and crannies up a large spiral that reached higher than seemed possible. Several branches jutted out from the shelves, almost like stepping stones to climb up the tower.

Steward fluttered down on the highest branch. "Oh, Bev, be right down!"

He let out another chirp as he hopped from branch to branch, descending down the tower until he landed near where she stood. Bev took a step back to allow him space, and he smiled—as much as possible for a beak.

"So glad to see you again," he said. "I've been hoping to cross paths with you. Hear you've been causing all kinds of trouble in Lower Pigsend lately!"

"Have you now?" Bev let out a humorless chuckle. "What kinds of trouble, specifically?"

"Well, first Nog was all up in arms about you," Steward said. "I'm afraid he caught sight of you and Merv coming out of my shop and wanted to know everything. I couldn't lie to him, nor did I know about the talisman yet, so I told him who you were."

Thanks for that... "It's fine," Bev said. "I did nothing wrong, as he finally figured out."

"Indeed," Steward said. "After he decided you *weren't* responsible, he's been running around town, destroying property and acting like he's doing it in search of the talisman. He's convinced it's still in town."

"How can he be sure?" Bev asked.

"I don't know," he replied with a shrug that loosened a few feathers from his wing. "But I do know he was in here, asking me to look up what kind of spell causes sneezing fits. Did you hear how it was stolen? Everyone just started sneezing one minute, then the talisman was just gone."

"I did," Bev said. "Did you have an answer for him?"

"No. I told him to speak with Percival, as that's not my area of expertise," he said with a chuckle. "I may have all this knowledge at my disposal, but it's not available to me at the drop of a hat like that wizard!"

Bev sincerely doubted that was the case now, but she didn't voice that thought.

"And speaking of, I've been poring over books, searching night and day for information on that amulet you gave me. It's quite tricky!"

"Oh dear, I'm so sorry," Bev said. "If it's too much—"

He waved a wing and hopped forward. "Nonsense. I'm nothing if not passionate about my dedication to the subject of research. I've determined the language is perhaps elven, but—"

"Elven?" Bev's brows shot upward. "As in *elves*? Goodness me."

"I'm not quite sure that's the case, though. Still trying to find exactly the right translation." He chuckled. "Been a long time since I've had a research project this complex. I must say it's keeping me up all hours of the night."

Bev forced a smile. "I'm happy to be rid of the amulet, to be honest. It would be quite all right with me if you never found out what it was."

"Oh, nonsense." Another bird-like chirp. "I love a good challenge. Even if it is to a topsider who took our talisman." He adjusted his suspenders. "I kid, I kid. I don't think it was you. After all, what would you need our talisman for?"

"Why do you think someone would've stolen it?" Bev asked. "I asked Percival yesterday—"

"Percival! You certainly have been all over the place, haven't you?" He hopped forward and back again. "What did Ol' Percy say about it?"

"Not much," Bev said. "But he did mention someone might've taken it for their own gain. Perhaps to cast another spell? Any thoughts on that?"

"I can't imagine who in town would be that selfish," he said. "But you know, if Nog thinks it's still in town, that could very well be the case. Perhaps if we see ol' Gerry Rickshaw sans feathers, we might know who stole it!"

Bev started. "Gerry? You think he might've—"

"Oh, he's harmless. Bit too heavy-handed on the tinctures for my liking, so I make my own, but he's good enough for the rest of the folk down here."

"I heard a lot of conversations happening on my way here," Bev said. "Folks in town are anxious. They think the magic is about to run out."

"I'm quite sure Percival is working on a solution." The bird ruffled his tail. "We're very fortunate to have such a brilliant wizard at our disposal."

"Right. Erm." Bev cleared her throat. "When was the last time you actually spoke with Percival?"

"It's been a few years. Why?"

"No reason." Bev didn't want to burst his bubble.

"Oh, you know..." He tapped his wing to his chin. "That's an idea. I bet Percival could help me figure out what kind of amulet it is. I should perhaps pay him a visit once he gets a free moment."

Bev forced a smile. Percival wouldn't be able to tell his left hand from his right, let alone help solve the problem of the amulet's origins.

"I'm sure he would love to help," she said, after a moment. "Listen, I'm on my way to speak with the magistrate, but no one's been able to tell me much about him. I'm sure you've met with him plenty, right? What should I expect?"

"Oh, no, I've never met him."

Bev frowned. "Merv said you always answer questions for him."

"The only people from the magistrate's office I've worked with are Nog and Bola," he said.

"What can you tell me about him?" Bev asked. "How did he come to be the magistrate?"

"When the town first closed itself off," he began, "things were a bit hastily put together. People were trying to get their bearings and make the town their own. Percival was everywhere at once, making houses bigger, helping replicate food, that sort of thing. Everyone got along well, too, because they were all reeling from the war and having to uproot their lives." He paused, letting out a small chirp. "But as you can imagine, after a few years, people get complacent. So to quell any dustups and arguments between people, Percival named a magistrate and endowed him with the ability to keep the peace. Thus our dear friends Officers Nog and Bola were appointed to carry out his wishes."

"So..." Bev licked her lips, making sure she understood. "You're saying that everyone in town just accepted that there was this new nameless, faceless person who Percival designated and gave the power to enforce the peace."

"Yes, practically." He waved off her skeptical expression. "You know, Percival does so much for so many of us. He's the reason we're all able to live down here, away from the queen's prying eyes. If he told us all to jump, I'm sure we'd do it."

"I see." Bev rubbed her hands together. "So if I wanted to speak with him, I would go to the Merchant's House, right?"

"Oh, no. I'd just find Officer Nog and tell him. He'll be sure to convey the message."

"Unfortunately, the message is about Officer Nog," Bev said.

"Officer Bola, then."

"Is there no way I can just speak to him directly?" Bev asked. "And don't you find it odd that no one in town has?"

"Shamus has, I'm sure. If you don't want to talk with Officer Nog or Bola, then he'll be the one to help you," Steward said with an impatient clack of his beak. "Anyway. I've got to get back to work. These books won't read themselves! I'll be sure to let you know if I find out anything about your amulet."

And with that, he took off up the tower, disappearing through a window.

Chapter Sixteen

The Merchant's House was as busy as ever, and the line to see Percival wrapped around the space. But there was also a crowd surrounding Shamus, many of them holding bags and seemingly eager to have the wizard assistant let them out.

"We have to leave!" one elf cried. "It's not safe for us here if the magic is gone."

"The magic is fine," Shamus said, waving another person in the replication queue back. "We're working on a replacement. Nothing to worry about. Everything is just fine. Go back to your homes."

"How can you say that when the magic protecting us is about to run out?"

"We demand to speak to the magistrate!"

"The wizard should come out and speak with us!"

"Percival is quite busy," Shamus said, "Keeping everyone fed and happy, if you recall. But I assure you, he's also very concerned about the missing talisman. It's why he and the magistrate sent Officer Bola in search of a new one. I have faith he'll be back any day now with news and a new talisman."

Bev's gaze landed on the square, where the talisman had been. Nog had said a few days ago that Bev had until Bola returned to solve the mystery of the second tunnel. Surely, he wouldn't be back yet. Not as if there were talismans just hanging around the countryside anymore.

The crowd continued to jeer and complain, pushing closer to Shamus, who was still waving the queue past while keeping the angry crowd at bay.

Bev marched right up to him and put her hands on her hips, announcing, "I'd like to speak with the magistrate."

At once, the crowd turned to look at her, and Bev got the distinct impression they knew exactly who she was and what she was doing there.

"What could you have to speak with him about?" Shamus asked, waving another person forward.

"That's my business," Bev said, not wanting to make things worse for Shamus by announcing to the crowd that she had evidence of illegal contraband, and that the magistrate's own man might be responsible.

"Then I guess it's not important enough to speak to the magistrate," Shamus said, turning away from her.

"I'd rather not say in front of the crowd," Bev pressed. "If you get my meaning."

"The magistrate, like Percival, is quite busy. Can't be stopping to speak with people who might be the cause of all the trouble."

"Well, if she's the cause of all the trouble, why is she still here?" an elf asked.

"Yeah, how come she can leave and we can't?"

"There's something you aren't telling us, isn't there, Shamus?"

"Is the spell already gone?"

"Are we unprotected?"

"What if the queen's people—"

"*Enough!*"

Shamus's voice echoed through the room, perhaps magically enhanced, as he'd pulled out his wand and the tip of it was glowing. The crowd quieted, staring at him as if he had two heads. Even Bev found herself without words, but more out of shock for the mild-mannered apprentice than because of some magical spell.

"Everything is *fine*," Shamus said, his voice strained as he gazed upon the crowd. "We've been able to patch things up for now. The magic is strong in the meantime. Percival is working on a long-term solution. The queen's people don't even know where we are. And if they did," Shamus caught Bev's gaze, "they'd come across the barrier spell and be turned away. There's no need to worry."

Whether by their own will or by magic, the angry part of the crowd dispersed, some grumbling about Shamus's tricks, leaving only the unbothered queue, who were just eager to get their wares duplicated by the wizard.

"Go on," Shamus said, gesturing to the next person in line. "Who's next?"

"I believe I'm next," Bev said. "As I do need to speak with the magistrate."

"You don't need to *do* anything," Shamus said with a grunt. "You're not from here. You need to go back to where you came from. No need to make everyone more antsy than you already have."

"You're threatening my friend," Bev said. "Just this morning, Officer Nog was harassing him, telling him that he alone is responsible for what's going on in Lower Pigsend."

"Well, he is." Shamus waved another person through. "If he hadn't dug that tunnel—"

Bev reached into her pocket and revealed the barley. "Then why did I find this barley in Lonny's basement? Percival said he wasn't the one who replicated it. Barley would've gone bad the past five years. So clearly, someone's bringing it in from the surface. And it's *certainly* not Merv."

Shamus eyed the barley and—to Bev's gaze—didn't seem surprised by it. "And what do you think the magistrate will do about it?"

"You've got another tunnel leading in, as I suspected, and I'm quite sure that your own people know about it, including and especially Officer Nog." She huffed. "And I'd hope that with all these people counting on them, they'd want to do something about it."

Shamus worked his jaw, before his attention turned back to the next person waiting in line, a squat woman with frazzled gray hair who carried what appeared to be a living plant that snapped at the air. He thumbed toward Percival, and she hurried inside.

"You'll need an appointment," he said, after a moment. "Come back tomorrow."

"I highly doubt that," Bev said. "Come on, Shamus. There's no need for all this subterfuge."

He worked his jaw. "Over there. That door will lead you where you want to go."

Bev followed his gaze and found a pair of doors she hadn't noticed before. Or had they not been there until Shamus said something?

"Thank you," Bev said, turning on her heel.

The doors opened, revealing a long, empty hall. Bev walked, straining her ears to hear conversations or other footsteps or anything, but the only sound were her own boots clacking on the ground. Up ahead, there was a corner, then another corner, then another.

Then she found herself standing at the entrance again. "Huh."

She turned on her heel and followed the same path again, and once again, after taking several corners, she found herself at the front doors.

"What in the...?" She put her hand to her head, turning around to march back into the maze.

This time, she turned this way, and that way, three lefts, two rights, and was right back at the front door before she could even count.

Bev walked out the front doors, the din of the Merchant's House coming back in full force. An elf walked by, and Bev flagged him down.

"Pardon," she said. "Do you know how to find the magistrate?"

He shook his head and kept walking.

Bev was getting the distinct impression something was amiss here. The doors hadn't even been visible until Shamus had said something, and it seemed to be one long hallway designed to befuddle and confuse people. Why would such a thing be necessary for the magistrate?

Unless... Bev's gaze narrowed as she realized Shamus was no longer directing people in and out of Percival's room. Officer Nog was there, his green, knobby hands clinging to Shamus's clipboard. His gaze plastered on Bev until she had no choice but to approach him.

"What are you doing down here?" he snapped.

"Trying to get answers," Bev said. "Isn't that what you charged me to do?"

"I told you to get me the name of the man selling tanddaes, which you've *yet* to do." He examined the elf's wooden shoes in front of him. "Go on back."

"I'm trying to speak with the magistrate," Bev said. "Where might I find him?"

Nog thumbed toward the door Bev had just exited from. "In there."

"Tried that. Seems like it's got an enchantment on it."

"So it would seem."

Bev pursed her lips. "Is there even a magistrate?"

"Of course there is," he snapped. "What, do you think we just fabricated him out of thin air? Made him up? You've got quite the imagination, lady."

"Then why was I just sent on a wild goose chase through a hallway that didn't have an end?" Bev said, gesturing toward the space she'd come from. "And now I find you here in Shamus's place. Almost like he was trying to avoid speaking with me again."

"Well, I *reckon* it's because there's some annoying topsider who's walking about town, asking questions that she doesn't need to know the answer to," Nog said. "And perhaps he wanted a few minutes to eat some lunch. Is that a crime?"

"No, but—"

"Then I suggest you head back to that inn and leave us be," Nog said. "Because it's not like you have anything *important* to tell the magistrate anyway."

Bev glared at him, her suspicions growing stronger that there wasn't actually a magistrate, and Shamus and Nog were somehow in cahoots to create a fictitious judge overseeing the law in town.

"Well? If you've got a question for the wizard, get in line and wait your turn like the rest of the crowd." He sidestepped her. "Next please."

"I'm not done—"

"I think you are," Nog said. "I said, *next*, ple— Oh. Gerry." His expression fell as the large chicken stepped forward, carrying nothing but a look of fury on his feathered face. "What do you need?"

Gerry flung a wing at Nog, leaving a trail of feathers on the ground. "To speak with *someone* about the lies going on in this town!"

Both Nog and Bev stared at him, shocked.

"What lies are you talking about?" Nog asked.

"The ones where that dastardly wizard apprentice *promised* he'd turn me human if I only provided him with the tinctures to keep Percival from keeling over!" Gerry barked, his words echoing around them and earning curious looks from those in line.

A small voice piped up from the floor, where a small mouse wearing an apron looked up nervously. "Percival is ill?" came her sweet little voice.

The pig-snouted man behind her gasped. "Percival is ill?"

"Percival is sick?"

"What are we going to do about the magic?"

"What about—"

"He's *fine*," Nog said, needing no magic to quell the crowd, only his sneer and his bark. "Now, Gerry, Shamus will come to visit you at your shop when he's got time."

"Time, eh? When does he have time? Only when he needs something, I tell you that much." Gerry was now leaving a trail of feathers as he paced in front of an agitated Nog. "Ask, ask, ask, that's all he does. Doubtful the man has a lick of magic of his own, always using his master's magic as cover. Never once has he given me a straight answer! I've half a mind to just stop making him tinctures, but how will I run my business if I can't get supplies?"

"That's *enough*, Gerry," Nog said. But his gaze wasn't on Bev, or even Gerry—it was squarely focused on the line of people watching the exchange with interest. "As soon as Shamus is back, I'll be sure to send him your way. You can *speak* with him then, and *I'm sure* he'll be more than happy to do whatever it is you want him to do."

Gerry glared at him, but seemed to understand that he wasn't going to get what he wanted out of the goblin. So with a loud *harrumph* and a spin that left even more feathers in his wake, he turned and stormed off.

Bev stood for a moment, looking between Nog and the trail of feathers Gerry had left, then dashed after the latter.

~

"What was that about?" Bev asked, walking up beside the half-chicken. "What kind of tinctures are you making for Percival?"

"Oh, um. Hello, Bev." Gerry's beady eyes ducked away as he picked up his pace. "Nothing. Just some vitamins to help with the lack of sun."

"Is that it?" Bev asked, lengthening her strides to keep up with him. "Because when I went in to see him yesterday, he was in a bad way. Are you sure—"

"It's fine," Gerry snapped, his beak flapping at her. "No need to trouble yourself with it. Don't you have an inn to run or something like that?"

"I do, but I'm also trying to figure out what in the world is going on down here," Bev said. "You said Percival is sick. I saw him myself and was very concerned about it. I'd like to know what else you know." She gestured toward the Merchant's House. "I just tried to see the magistrate, and *somebody* sent me around and around in a hallway that never ended. I'm not really sure there *is* a magistrate."

"That's a fine theory," Gerry said. "You should talk to someone else about it."

"I think Percival is a victim, too." Bev jogged to keep up with him. "His apprentice either hasn't noticed or doesn't care that he's one strong wind away from keeling over. And now I find out you've been making him tinctures? What was it that Shamus promised you in return? To turn you human?"

Gerry glanced behind him, scowling, and for a moment, Bev was sure he was going to argue with her. But instead he grabbed her by the arm and yanked her into an alley.

"Yes, all right?" he whispered harshly. "Shamus came to me a few years ago and asked me to put together some potions for his health and sanity. Mages aren't meant to give so much of themselves, you know? So I told him I'd make him tinctures and keep it quiet, but on one condition: that he figure out a way to fix this problem." He gestured to himself. "Shamus said he'd look into it. So I made potions, and kept asking about my payment. Every time, he had some excuse. 'I'm busy' or 'It's a complex spell, having the bird scribe look into it.' And like an idiot, I believed him instead of seeing what it really was—another of Shamus's lies."

"So what's changed?"

"Well, the talisman, obviously! If it's gone, there's nothing stopping the queen's people from marching down here and rounding up the lot of us, myself included. No telling what they'd think of these feathers." He huffed. "I figure, after all I've done for him, he should do me a solid. But every time I even walk into the Merchant's House these days, that goblin's standing there instead. I think Shamus has a spell on the place to look out for me."

"Do you think they're actually going to be able to find a replacement?" Bev asked.

He scoffed. "Doubtful. Even if they did find a talisman just *lying* around, someone would have to cast another spell, and I don't know if Shamus has that kind of magic up his sleeve. I've never seen him use any, but maybe that's because he doesn't want to lose his mind like his boss." He shrugged. "Still, if he thinks I'm going to let myself be arrested after busting my tailfeathers to keep Percival going, he's got another think coming!"

And with that, he stormed off, leaving a trail of feathers in his wake.

Bev had a strong urge to keep following him, but the clock in the town square chimed. Two o'clock in the afternoon. Her time today was up.

Chapter Seventeen

Although someone was watching the inn, Bev still hurried back, both eager to find out how the kids had done and dreading it. She said a quick hello and goodbye to Merv, promising to give him a full report in the morning then continued through the tunnel.

She braced herself. Her bread, she'd already told herself, was probably going to be a disaster. The overnight batch *might* be all right, but there was a good chance it was overproofed and gloppy. The batch she'd made this morning was probably less of a mess, but only if she could catch it before the kids started shaping it. Three o'clock was a bit late to be getting it in baskets for the second rise, but if she needed to do that, she would.

Dinner itself, she was a bit more optimistic about. Ida and Vellora would've certainly gotten the kids squared away with the right cut of meat, and perhaps given guidance on how to cook it correctly.

Really, though, the only thing Bev was hoping for was that there would be guests at the inn, and she'd be able to collect some coin for the first time in a few days.

Bev pushed open the front door, and her heart sank. No one was there to greet her. "Hello?" she called. "PJ? Valta? Grant? Biscuit? Anyone here?"

She closed the door behind her, and the delicious aroma of dinner hit her nose. Well, at least they hadn't failed her there.

"Hello?" she called, walking toward the kitchen. "Anyone here?"

There was a thump from upstairs, followed by footsteps. PJ appeared on the landing, Biscuit at his heels. The laelap's tail wagged ferociously, and he took the stairs two-by-two to greet her. She knelt and scratched the base of his tail, earning a wiggle from him.

"Welcome back," PJ said with a smile.

"Thank you," Bev said, looking around. "Where are your friends?"

He rubbed the back of his head. "They...um... decided they had better things to do. Left around midday when there was nothing to do and haven't come back."

Bev considered having a word with their guardians, but thought better of it. They were volunteering, after all. And she'd only have to fork over one half a silver instead of three. "So you've been here all by yourself?"

He nodded. "For a bit. They stuck around while I finished all the chores and errands." He cleared his throat as he ticked off his fingers. "I brought the flour back, and refilled your canister in the kitchen, and put the rest in your root cellar. I went to the farmer's market and found Alice, who was delighted to see me again and…uh…*didn't* mention that I'd destroyed her barn a few weeks ago."

"She certainly wouldn't know that," Bev said with a kind smile.

"Anyway, she helped me with the produce, and gave me a pint of her early season blueberries, just in case you could find something to do with those," he said.

"I'm sure I can."

"She also sold me a large crate of root vegetables, and I put those in your root cellar." He paused. "Except for the ones I pulled out to make dinner. I went over to the butchers', and Ida sold me a slab of beef. Helped me get the oven to the right temperature then helped me get your herbs. She said you usually use thyme and rosemary in your beef, along with a little wine, so we did that. She wasn't sure how much you usually use, so I did a couple sprigs. Hope that's all right."

Emotion welled in Bev's chest as he spoke, grateful so many had stepped up to help in her time of need. Even if she didn't have any guests, at least she knew she could count on the folks in town, and that was worth its weight in gold.

"Oh, and..." He reached into his pocket and handed her four gold coins. "You've got four guests upstairs. I was just settling the last of them."

She gasped. "PJ, you've done amazing. I can't even begin to thank you for all you did today."

"Well, you should hold your praise until you see what dinner and the bread looks like," he said with a small blush.

"All right, then. Let's go check it out."

The kitchen was spotless, and as Bev pulled her baking dish from the oven and revealed the roast cooking inside, she inhaled the scent of the herbs. It smelled divine, and looked to be perfectly timed, needing just a few more hours to be tender.

"Excellent work." Bev turned to scan the kitchen. "What about the bread?"

"Well, I think I did all right." He beckoned her to follow. "Here's the batch from this morning, you said."

He pulled the tea towel from three nicely-risen loaves in the proofing baskets. Bev tapped their tops, finding them nearly ready for the oven. The shape left a little to be desired, and they might come out a little flat, but they'd certainly taste up to even Etheldra's standards.

"And the other ones?" Bev asked.

"Oh, well." His blush deepened. "I know you said we weren't supposed to bake them, but they looked awfully puffy and doubled. Allen said I had to worry about them getting *too* puffy, so he told me to go ahead and put them in the oven. I pulled them out about half an hour ago."

He led her to the other side of the kitchen, and Bev held her breath as he pulled off the tea towel. But the loaves were brown and perfectly-shaped.

"Wow, I really didn't think that was going to work," Bev said. "I suppose the proof is in the taste, but they certainly look like my usual bread."

"You aren't mad I went ahead and baked them?" he asked. "They're getting cold."

"Well, you do have to let them cool all the way before cutting into them," Bev said. "And I can always pop them in the oven for a few minutes before serving, just to warm them up again." She reached for her knife. "But since we have so much bread…how's about we test them and compare? I confess, I'm a bit eager to find out the differences."

"What do you mean?" PJ asked.

She explained how she was tweaking her bread recipe every day to make it the best it could possibly be, and last night's experiment was to let it ferment longer in a colder environment. With a smile, she pulled out a knife and sliced through one of the overnight breads, inhaling the yeasty, rosemary scent.

Then Bev offered the slice to the teenager. "You get the first taste."

"Are you sure?" PJ asked.

"You baked them." She offered it again. "Try it."

He took the bread from her, inhaling it and inspecting it as she'd done. Then, with another nervous look at her, he took a bite, chewing thoughtfully. "Not sure what I'm looking for, but it certainly tastes all right. Pretty good, I'd say." He paused, laughing nervously. "It's bread. It's delicious, of course, but it's…well, it's bread."

Bev had to give him that. Etheldra, Earl, and Bardoff had been eating her bread for years, so they were keen to the differences. They'd certainly have more to say.

"Why don't you try some?" PJ asked.

"I'll save my piece for dinner, so I can compare it with the one baking in the oven," Bev said. "Are you staying for dinner?"

"No. I've got to be getting home," PJ said. "I told my mom I'd be by to help clean up the shop."

"Go on," Bev said, nodding to the door. "And give her my thanks for all your help today. You don't know how much it means to me. And four guests? That certainly makes me a happy innkeeper." She hesitated. "Are you...willing to come back tomorrow? I'll pay you a silver-and-a-half for your trouble." After all, he was more than worth the price of his two friends, too.

"If you'll have me," he said with a smile. "This is the easiest money I've ever made. Sure beats picking up tossed horseshoes with my parents."

~

After PJ left, Bev walked upstairs to introduce herself to her four guests—Mr. and Mrs. Yancey, Ms. Page, and Mr. Norville. They were all travelers of various backgrounds, the usual fare for the Weary Dragon. All coming from different directions and going in different directions. Nothing too exciting about any of them, and for that, Bev was grateful. She couldn't handle any more excitement.

At six on the nose, Bev brought out dinner, plating her bread in two different baskets. The four guests were ecstatic to see the food, but none were as happy as Earl, who was the first of the regulars to arrive.

"I was worried Etheldra'd give me another earful if there was barley soup," he said. "That's a lot of bread there, Bev."

"Well, I managed a little experiment today," she said, offering him both baskets. "This is the regular batch, and this is one I let ferment in my root cellar overnight."

"Oh?" He put a regular piece on one side of his

plate and the experiment on the other. "Well, I'm excited to taste them."

Bardoff and Etheldra were similarly curious about her experiment, with Etheldra giving her an earful about finally taking her innkeeping duties seriously. Bev let her tirade, as it made the tea shop owner happy, and said nothing in response.

"Hoping you prefer the overnight version," Bev said to the three once they were seated. "It would certainly make my morning chores a bit easier."

"Harrumph. Well, if they're in the service of helping you *skirt* by, I don't see how it…" She took a bite and her grey eyebrows shot up.

Bev held her breath—Etheldra was nothing if not blunt—and waited for the verdict.

"This is…"

"Amazing!" Earl said, taking a bite of the other bread to compare. "Oh, yes. For sure," he said with his mouth full. "Much improved. The overnight proof is a winner!"

"I quite agree." Bardoff nodded firmly. "It's quite flavorful. Complex, even. Definitely a winner."

The four guests, none of whom had tasted Bev's bread before, seemed to agree. "I'm not sure what it tasted like before," Ms. Page said. "But this might the the best bread I've ever had in my life!"

Considering her age, that was quite the compliment. But the only one who hadn't spoken yet was Etheldra, who was still chewing with a look of consternation on her face. She swallowed with purpose and turned to Bev.

"I saw that young PJ with Sin and your wagon today," she said, clearly wanting to drag this out. "What was that about?"

"Oh, he kept the inn for me today," Bev said. "Got all the produce, the meat, tended to the bread. Greeted my guests." She nodded to the four. "I'm very grateful for his help today. And everyone else who stopped in to give him a hand."

"He's a delightful young man," Mr. Yancey, who'd come in from the west and was going east, said.

His wife, a snowy-haired woman with a kind smile, nodded emphatically. "Quite."

"Hmph. A little too mischievous for my tastes," Etheldra said with a snort. "Don't like his friends, either."

"I take it your little adventure still isn't finished?" Earl asked Bev.

"I wish," she said with a sigh. "Just when I think I've got a handle on things, someone knocks it out of kilter again."

"Bev is our resident mystery solver," Bardoff explained to the four newcomers. "Though we never did figure out what was causing all those building implosions recently."

"Goodness me, building implosions?" Mr. Norville put a hand to his chest.

"Oh, yes," Earl said with a solemn nod. "My workshop, Alice's barn, the schoolhouse."

"Don't forget the seamstress shop," Etheldra said.

"Scary times, for sure," Earl said. "Kept me busy! But nothing's happened in a few weeks, so that's been nice." He chuckled. "Maybe it *was* those grannies, Bev!"

"Maybe so," Bev said with a neutral shrug.

"So you've got a new mystery?" Bardoff asked.

"Something like that," Bev said. "It's a bit of an odd one."

"Can we help?" Bardoff asked.

She shook her head. "I feel like I'm at the end of it, which is good. Don't like leaving the inn all day, even if I *do* have a wonderful assistant in young PJ." She paused, eyeing Etheldra, who was nibbling on the bread again. "I'm still waiting for your verdict, Etheldra. Which bread do you prefer?"

Etheldra took her time tasting both pieces, considering them, then repeating the action two or three more times. Bev got the distinct impression she was enjoying the bated-breath attention. But finally, after a *very* long silence, she spoke.

"While I disagree with *anything* that will divert your attention away from your job, I have to cede that the new version is much more flavorful."

Bev grinned as Earl and Bardoff rose in a standing ovation. Mr. Norville joined in, though based on his face, he was merely following the suggestion of the crowd, not because he knew what was going on.

Etheldra let out her trademark *harrumph*. "I said it's better, but it's not an excuse to ignore your duties. You'd better *wrap it up* and get back to work soon."

"Plan on it."

~

In the morning, Bev wanted to stay at the inn long enough to see off her customers. They were once again complimentary of the inn, of dinner, and, very specifically, of PJ's attention to them and making them feel welcome. Allen hadn't yet come by, but they all insisted they had to be on their way. By seven in the morning, when Allen arrived with a basket of blueberry muffins, the inn was once again deserted, and Bev had finished her morning chores.

"Oh goodness, sorry I'm a little late," he said with a frown. "Got waylaid trying to bake for a birthday party and lost track of time."

"You could probably use some help," Bev said. "When I'm done with PJ, I'll be sure to send him over to you."

"I doubt he'd want to wake up early," Allen said with a shake of his head. "Goodness knows Grant doesn't. I was afraid his eyes would get stuck in his skull from the eye roll he gave me when I asked."

Bev laughed. "Well, he and Valta didn't stick

around here yesterday. But PJ… Thank you so much for bringing him here and having him help."

"I'm glad he worked out, but I'm a little miffed about Grant. You know, soon Vicky's going to be moving in with me above the bakery, and out of the apartment above Apolinary's shop. Grant needs to find a place to live, and to do that, he needs a job. So he really shouldn't be so cavalier about it."

"What happened to him helping Earl out?" Bev asked.

"Short-lived," he said. "Too much hard work for him, he said. Got one too many splinters and quit."

Bev tutted. "That's a shame. Earl probably could've used an apprentice. But good for you for keeping an eye on him."

"As much as I hate to admit it," Allen said, "Grant's going to be my problem as soon as Vicky and I marry. There's no one else around to keep him straight, and he's still a kid, you know? Just wish he'd be a little less sullen about it all."

"If I recall correctly, you were a bit sullen after your mother's passing, too," Bev said with a kind smile. "Maybe you're kindred spirits."

"Maybe." He pushed the muffins toward her. "I'm glad PJ's pulling his weight. Did the bread turn out all right? I usually leave that sort of thing to you."

"Brilliant. Etheldra couldn't find fault with it," Bev said.

"Oh goodness, that is high praise. Maybe we should throw a party?" Allen chuckled.

"Well, I'm not sure if it was the skill of your baking or my abysmal performance the night before," Bev said. "Should've just thrown out that bread, but..."

"Are you sure you're all right?" Allen said. "I'm worried about you. It's not like you to be gone from the inn so much. You've certainly got to have some ideas on how to solve this mystery now, don't you?"

"I wish I did," Bev said. "Yesterday, I attempted to bring my evidence to the magistrate in Lower Pigsend. I was sent down a long tunnel, full of twists and turns, and no ending. Nobody else was there, either. Just wandering around like I had nowhere to be." She huffed. "Seemed like an enchantment, but when I went to confront the wizard's apprentice, he was gone and that nasty little goblin was there in his place—Officer Nog. I've got it on good authority that *he's* just making things up to frame Merv, perhaps blaming him for his own failings. I don't think it was a coincidence he was waiting for me after I'd asked about the magistrate."

"So you think he's keeping you away from his boss?" Allen asked.

"No, actually," Bev said with a sigh, "I don't think there *is* a magistrate. The whole thing just seems so unbelievable. But I fear if there isn't someone to report Nog's horrendous behavior to..."

How am I supposed to help Merv?"

"Sounds like a pickle," Allen said.

The door opened, and PJ walked inside, rubbing sleep from his eyes and plastering on a bright smile. "Morning, Bev. Allen. How did dinner go last night?"

"Perfect," Bev said. "You've got a future in innkeeping, I think."

"Are you headed back to Lower Pigsend?" PJ asked.

Bev nodded, sharing a look with Allen. "I haven't a clue what I'm going to do next, but maybe Merv has some ideas. He always does." She picked up the basket of muffins. "And I'm sure he won't mind these, either."

Chapter Eighteen

Bev arrived at Merv's house at half past nine, and he was, indeed, happy to receive the blueberry muffins.

"I'm sure they're delicious. They probably won't put you to sleep, either," Bev said with a laugh. "But I'm glad to see you in better spirits this morning. Officer Nog hasn't been by yet, has he?"

"No, thank goodness. Then again, I'm not sure I would've noticed if he had," he said. "I snuck one of Lillie's cookies last night and…well, I just woke up. Best night I've had in ages."

"I'm happy to hear that, at least," Bev said. "You really must keep your strength up."

"What's the latest with the investigation?"

Bev told him of her adventures the day before, of Gerry's suspicions about Shamus, and of her own hunch that this infamous magistrate didn't actually exist. Merv's proverbial eyebrows rose at that last admission.

"*That* would be a scandal, for sure," Merv said. "But who'd go through all that trouble to make up a fake magistrate?"

"Nog seems like he would," Bev said. "And if he and Shamus are in cahoots..."

"You should go talk with Lillie," Merv said. "She's much smarter about how things work in Lower Pigsend than I am." He yawned. "And kind. And—" His snout drooped for a second before popping back up. "Goodness me."

"Merv, did you eat another cookie?" Bev asked, putting her hands on her hips.

"Please, take them from me." He handed her the box. "Otherwise, I'll be sure to snooze the day away."

Bev tossed the box of cookies in the first bin she came across in town. She hated to throw out Lillie's hard work, but she didn't want to think about what Nog would say if he showed up at Merv's and the moleman was fast asleep.

Even before Bev opened the door to the bakery, the aroma of sweet and spice and nuts made her mouth water. Inside, Lillie was tending to her oven, her apron covered in flour and icing as she whirled around the space.

"Oh, Bev, good morning," Lillie said. "I was just working on these cookies for Merv. I'm sure he's already eaten the box from yesterday."

Bev didn't have the heart to tell her she'd tossed them. "Are you sure he needs more? You've baked him so many."

"Well, if I don't, I'll have to make room for more of his anxiety blankets," Lillie said, nodding to a chair in the corner that held at least ten of Merv's blankets. "And I'm running out of space. A little calm, and perhaps he can pare down to his usual output."

"I understand that," Bev said. "Perhaps, though, you might tweak the recipe."

"Why?" She paused and pursed her lips before her face fell. "Don't tell me it knocked him out again. I swear, I adjusted the magic. It's *barely* there."

"Whatever you've put in them seems to work quite well to put him to sleep," Bev said. "Not that Merv's complaining. He told me it was the best rest he's gotten in a while. But you know, perhaps not the time for that. What with Nog wandering about and threatening things."

Lillie's eyes lit up in recognition then concern. "Goodness me, I didn't even think. It's a good thing Nog hasn't seen him while he's fast asleep from a cookie." She walked the fresh pan of cookies from the oven and tossed them in the trash. "Well, I'll just have to make him some regular cookies without any sort of calming added to it." She pursed her lips. "That apothecary probably gave me a carrier potion that was way too strong."

"Gerry?" Bev asked, and Lillie nodded. "What's a carrier potion?"

"Well, for something like a calming magic, I need a little help to keep the magic inside the confection," she said. "Gerry made a tincture that I add to the dough. But I'm sure he made it far too strong. He's not the best apothecary, but we make do with what we have."

"Is he the only one in town?" Bev asked.

"As far as I'm aware," she replied. "Otherwise, I'd be talking to them instead of that chicken. Bad enough he always gets feathers in my potions."

"He was furious at Nog and Shamus yesterday," Bev said, tapping her finger against her chin. "Accused Shamus of failing to turn him into a human. Apparently, he's been making tinctures for Percival for years to keep him healthy. But if they're anything like your carrier potion, perhaps he's not the right person to be making them."

"And probably explains why Percival's on his last legs, as you say," Lillie said with a sigh. "But he's not the only one getting antsy. The talisman magic is about to run out, and they're no closer to finding a replacement. Meanwhile, Nog is harassing almost every business he can get his grubby little fingers into, saying he's still looking for the original talisman. I saw him at a cobbler yesterday. What would a cobbler need with a talisman?" She shook her head. "I think you were on to something about them framing Merv for their own failures."

"Well, I'd love to tell his boss, but when I tried to meet with the magistrate, I was given the runaround. I figured Nog was hiding something, but now I'm convinced it's quite large, and he's working with Shamus."

"Shamus?" She frowned. "Percival's assistant?"

Bev nodded, telling her about yesterday's mishap. "And when I come out, who should be there but Officer Nog. I'm convinced the magistrate doesn't actually exist."

Lillie let out a laugh. "Oh, Bev. Of course he exists."

"Does he, though?" Bev asked. "Have you seen him?"

Her pale cheeks reddened. "Well, no. I don't even know his name. Just know he's somewhere—"

"The Merchant's House," Bev finished for her. "You don't have regular town meetings or anything like that?"

"Where would we fit all the people?" she said with a giggle. "As far as I know, most of the magistrate's edicts come from Nog and Bola bothering people." She paused, giving Bev a look. "People are just happy to be safe down here, Bev. Even if the magistrate is made up, the thought of him has done what's needed. We're all safe, aren't we?"

"I don't know about that," Bev said. "Nog is terrorizing the town without any check on his power, Shamus seems to be letting him, and neither one cares that poor Percival is on his last legs."

"Oh, Percival's a bit flighty, but—"

Bev put her hand on her hip. "He's downright ill, Lillie. And Shamus and the rest don't seem to care."

She closed her mouth, seemingly taken aback by Bev's tone.

"Sorry. It just bothered me to see him," Bev said, adjusting her shirt distractedly. "What do you think I should do about the magistrate?"

"I don't know," Lillie said. "Shamus controls access to Percival, and he's the only other person in town who might be able to rein in Nog." She paused. "You said you saw Gerry talking with them yesterday?"

Bev nodded. "I wouldn't call it talking, more like threatening."

"I—" Lillie stopped, looking toward the door as if she'd heard something. "That's odd."

"What?"

"I've been summoned," she said.

"Summoned?" Bev looked left then right. "Summoned how?"

"Magically," Lillie said, undoing her apron. "Everyone in town has."

Sure enough, across the street, people walked outside, staring at each other with the same confused look that Lillie wore, all of them walking toward the center of town. Lillie crossed the shop to stand in the doorway, brow furrowed as she watched the street for a minute.

"Who summoned you?" Bev asked.

"Only two people have that sort of power," she said with a chuckle. "It must be important. They've never done anything like this before, you know."

Bev craned her neck to look down the street. "What do you think it's about?"

"Haven't a clue. But if I don't head that way, this knocking in my mind is going to drive me batty. So we might as well go see what Shamus wants."

~

Bev and Lillie followed the crowd as it coalesced in front of the Merchant's House. There were certainly a *lot* of creatures gathered, but standing on the front steps were Shamus and Officer Nog. Shamus wore a wizard's outfit, similar to Percival's, and Nog was hopping from one foot to the other, glaring at the crowd as if they'd personally offended him.

"This is strange," Lillie said as the crowd filled in behind them. "Everyone in town is here. I don't think I've ever seen anything like this before."

The crowd was thick with people, from the small mice to the tall elves to the fairies flying overhead. Even Steward flew down and perched on a lamppost, eagerly ruffling his feathers. Bev scanned the space, looking for Gerry, and couldn't find him.

"Attention, everyone." Shamus's voice echoed over the space. "Please, quiet down. We have an announcement to make."

The murmurs took a while to quiet, and Bev mused that Shamus perhaps could benefit from Mayor Hendry's unique brand of magic to manage the crowds.

"Yes, well," Shamus began as soon as the bulk of the conversations had stopped. "As you all know, a few days ago, we had a bit of a scare with the talisman that keeps us safe."

"More than a scare!" came an angry cry from the audience.

"It was stolen!"

"Have you found it?"

"What happened to it?"

The voices echoed all at once, and it was hard to make out what anyone was saying. Shamus held out his hands to quiet them, but the crowd was in danger of becoming unruly. Lillie let out a cry as she was pushed forward, and Bev reached out to steady her.

"*Oi!*" Nog's voice echoed over the din. "*Quiet down, you lot!*"

That worked.

"Now," Shamus said, adjusting his shirt, "as I was saying. We had a scare, but you will all be pleased to know that Officer Nog found the talisman, and we're happy to report it's intact and fine."

A pail, looking much like the one that had been stolen, appeared next to Shamus and floated up over the crowd. Bev eyed it carefully, noting the way it glowed and sparkled, just like the old one had. Based on the expressions of the crowd, they were similarly impressed by it.

"So…we're safe?" someone in the crowd asked.

"No more worrying about the queen?"

"What about that tunnel?"

"What about the moleman?"

"What about who stole it?"

Shamus held up his hands, and once again, it was of no use. Nog had to bark at the crowd a few times, but they eventually quieted again.

"We will be handling the tunnel," Shamus said. "As it stands, the new talisman spells should be more than enough to keep the queen's people out, so there's no need to worry. But…" His gaze somehow landed on Bev. "We do know there are some *loopholes* that have recently come to light, and we'll be working with Percival to close them."

"And as for who *stole* the thing," Nog said, also catching Bev's gaze.

"Don't you dare say it was me," she muttered.

"It was *this* feathery fiend," Shamus said, holding his arm out. From inside the Merchant House, Bola walked out with...

"Gerry?" Bev said with a gasp and a shared look of confusion with Lillie. "Gerry stole it?"

"We were tipped off by the sneezing," Nog said. "He spread some of his tinctures in the area, causing the diversion and allowing him to take the talisman for himself."

"But why?" asked someone from the crowd.

"Gerry?" Shamus said, gesturing to him. "Why did you take it?"

"Because you promised me you'd turn me human," he said, anger on his feathered face. "And when you didn't, I decided to take matters into my own hands."

"Percival did say it was possible to cast a different spell on it," Bev said to Lillie. "But I can't believe... Gerry, of all people. Seems..."

Well, it seemed far-fetched, but perhaps Nog and Bola had more information than she did. And if they found the talisman on his person...

"I'm just glad we can put this whole messy episode behind us," Shamus said. "Please, return to your homes. All is well in Lower Pigsend now. No need to worry yourselves anymore." He turned to Gerry with a sneer. "We'll make sure this treacherous thief is *permanently* barred from our town."

~

The crowd dispersed, but Bev and Lillie hung around until they could get close enough to Nog. The goblin didn't seem eager to speak with them, lifting his lip in a curled sneer.

"Well? Seems we found our culprit. No thanks to your efforts," he said.

"However did you figure it out?" Bev asked.

"Found the talisman in his basement," Nog said. "Tipped me off when he came ranting and raving at Shamus yesterday. He tried to use it to turn himself human, and when it didn't work, he was going to blackmail Shamus into doing it. But he's not the cleverest chicken in the coop, so we were able to recover the talisman before any of that could happen."

"And Merv?" Bev asked.

Nog ground his teeth.

"Clearly, his tunnel isn't doing any harm," Bev pressed. "The talisman is back, everything is as it was, right? So no need to take any action against him."

Nog worked his knobby jaw. "Sure. We'll leave him alone. But if I catch *you* down here again—"

"No need." Bev held up her hands. "I have an

inn to run, and I'm very happy to be getting back to it."

~

Lillie walked Bev back to Merv's tunnel, and Bev found herself a little sad her time with Lillie was at an end.

"Well, it's not like I'll *never* see you again," Lillie said. "I'm sure I'll be by Merv's."

Bev laughed. "You know, maybe we can coordinate. Every third Tuesday, I'll bring you a sack of real flour, and you can bring me some cookies."

She licked her lips, nodding intently. "You know, that's not a bad idea. Maybe I'll just bake a cake and eat it all myself. What Officer Nog doesn't know won't hurt him."

"Maybe indeed." Bev held out her hand. "Thank you for all your help. I hope things can get back to normal down here."

"As normal as they ever get," Lillie replied, taking Bev's hand and squeezing it. "I'm sure it's only a matter of time before something else goes haywire."

"If it does, you'll be the one they call on, not me," Bev said. "I'm just lucky I have such dear friends to keep tabs on things for me back at the inn. But that's where I belong."

"Indeed you do." Lillie wiped away a tear. "Well…"

"Suppose it's time." Bev nodded, gazing on

Lower Pigsend with a satisfied sigh. "Goodbye, Lillie. It's been a pleasure."

"Likewise."

Chapter Nineteen

Bev had never been so happy to wake up the next morning and lie there for a moment. Biscuit was snoring quietly between her legs, and the sky was turning pink. Even though she hadn't been the one to solve the mystery, she still felt a sense of accomplishment. Merv's tunnel would remain open, the people of Lower Pigsend would be safe from the queen's people. Everything as it was.

Although she couldn't help but feel for Percival, and to a lesser extent, Lillie. Percival would continue scraping along, propped up by…well, not tinctures, since Gerry was presumably no longer selling them. Lillie had said there wasn't another apothecary in the town, so…

"Not my concern," Bev said, with a firm shake of her head.

Shamus seemed a smart fellow. He'd be able to figure it out himself. And Bev could focus on the inn.

Bev had told PJ she wouldn't need him today, and the young man had seemed a little disappointed. But she promised he was welcome to come give her a hand any time he felt like it.

She set to her chores at a leisurely pace, a far cry from the last few days of quickly moving through them. She made the bread the night before, curious if she could recreate the deliciousness of the overnight proof. Sin was glad to get her breakfast at what the mule most likely presumed a reasonable time. There was a single guest, and Bev saw them off, stripping their beds and tidying up before nine.

With the inn ready for the next evening, Bev settled onto her chair in the front room and took a moment to enjoy the peace once more.

Her thoughts drifted toward Merv, and Lillie, and Lower Pigsend. She hoped the baker had made another batch of cookies and delivered them to Merv to celebrate their good fortune. Bev would certainly miss the delectable sweets from the pobyd —though she did have a basket of muffins from Allen.

Around noon, Bev headed across the street to the butcher's, where she was greeted with more than a little sass from Ida.

"Well, aren't *you* a sight for sore eyes," she said with a look. "Was pretty sure you'd forgotten where we were."

"Har har," Bev said. "Thank you for helping PJ keep the inn."

"He's a good kid," Vellora chimed in from the back. "Eager to help. Almost like he owes you something." She gave Bev a knowing look. "Ida and I think he had something to do with those buildings coming down a few weeks ago."

"Well, if he does or doesn't, the buildings have stopped crashing, so there's nothing to discuss," Bev said with a half-shrug. Although the butchers wouldn't *ever* divulge the dragon shifter's secret to anyone who could hurt him, Bev wasn't keen to share it with anyone, just in case.

"Fine, don't tell us," Ida said with a mock pout. "We're just your dearest friends. At least tell me what happened in Lower Pigsend."

Bev shared the latest developments, including the arrest of Bernard's brother and how everything was put back, and Ida pouted again.

"Goodness, what an anticlimactic tale," she said. "You didn't even get to do your big reveal!"

"What?" Bev laughed.

"You know, where you get to find out what the villain was thinking?" Ida said. "And you get to save the day? Oh, it was so exciting when you got that

Bernie fellow to spill the beans."

Vellora scoffed. "You've got a weird definition of exciting, my love."

"No, I didn't get any of that," Bev said with a laugh. "It was more 'here's the bad guy, everything is fine. Go back to Pigsend, Bev, we've got everything covered now,'" Bev said, imitating Nog's gruff tone. "I can't say I'm sad not to go down there today. It took me at least half an hour both ways. And goodness knows the inn was feeling neglected."

"Still. What do you think they did to Bernard's brother?" Ida asked.

"Perhaps the same thing they were planning to do to Merv," Bev replied with a shrug. "I do need to check on him now that all this has blown over. But perhaps in a day or so."

"Yes, you deserve a rest," Ida said with a cheeky wink. "And speaking of, what's your meat order for this evening?"

~

Bev opted for a pork loin and decided to pair it with those blueberries PJ had gotten at the farmers' market the day before in a compote. As she worked, the kitchen filled with the most delectable smells. The sweetness of the blueberries got her thinking of the carrots Lillie used in her confections, so she made an extra side dish of roasted carrots with a dash of cinnamon.

Around four in the afternoon, as she was getting

her bread in the oven, the front door opened, and someone called out.

"Be right there," Bev called back, closing the oven door and taking off her apron. She walked out into the front room where a man stood by the front desk.

"Oh, good afternoon. I'd like to rent a room for the evening." He seemed somewhat familiar, but Bev couldn't place him. He was tall, with salt-and-pepper hair, a wide grin, and clothes that looked like they were made for a much larger person. The way he looked at Bev suggested that *he* knew *her*, but Bev hadn't the foggiest where she'd seen him before.

Bev flashed a smile. "Welcome to the Weary Dragon. Will you be staying with us for the night?"

"Appears so," he said, glancing out the door. "As it seems I'm not *welcome*..."

"Pardon?" Bev asked.

"Nothing." He walked up to her and stuck a hand in his pocket. "How much for the evening? Does it include dinner?"

"One gold, and it does."

He made a face. "Things are certainly more expensive than they used to be..."

"Used to be?" Bev asked.

"Nothing. Here." He slapped the coin down. "Happy to be moving on as soon as I can in the morning."

"Excellent. Room three for you." She handed

him the key, and he stuffed it in his pocket, still watching her with that curious expression. "What name should I put down for you?"

"Hm?"

"So I know what to call you," Bev said.

"Oh, it's um… Harold," he said.

"Harold." She jotted that down on the line next to *room three*. She'd been at this long enough to know that if someone didn't want to offer their last name, it was best not to pry. "Happy to have you with us for the evening. Dinner will be at six."

"Good." He turned to leave, but Bev couldn't help her curiosity.

"Pardon," Bev said. "Have we…met before? You look awfully familiar."

"I've just got one of those faces," he said over his shoulder, picking up his suitcase and walking up the stairs.

Bev winced as the door slammed, and looked down at Biscuit. "What do you suppose is his problem?"

Biscuit sniffed the ground where the man had been standing, but didn't indicate there was anything amiss there.

"Well, he's probably right. He just has one of those faces."

~

Bev couldn't wait to cut into her loaves, eager to taste the overnight proofing once more. The regulars arrived at six o'clock on the dot, and each one seemed excited for the spread Bev had laid out for them.

"This certainly looks like you put some effort into it," Earl said, helping himself to the loin and compote. "Glad to see you back at the inn. All good now?"

"I...think so," Bev said, a wary eye on the newcomer as he descended the stairs. "Hope so, anyway. Glad to be here for a day, at least."

"PJ help you out today?" Bardoff asked.

"No, I sent him back home," Bev replied. "But he's been an invaluable resource, you know. I've got to swing by his folks' house and thank them for letting him cover for me while I was away."

"He's a good kid," Bardoff said, his eyes widening as he took in the food. "This smells heavenly. Is that cinnamon on the carrots? How clever!"

"Wasn't my idea," Bev said.

Harold—though Bev was fairly sure that wasn't his name—queued behind Bardoff and helped himself to the food. Bev kept a wary eye on him as he plated more than a little food and took four slices of rosemary bread. He settled at one of the empty tables, not with the three Pigsend residents, and tucked in.

"Oh, my goodness," he muttered as soon as the first forkful entered his mouth.

"Bev is quite the excellent cook," Bardoff said, leaning over to nod at the traveler. "So, what did you say your name was?"

"Harold," he replied, his mouth full of food. "This is more than excellent. It's divine. Heavenly. Exquisite."

"Now calm down, you'll give Bev a complex." Etheldra glared at him over the tip of her nose. "And, while it is quite an improvement from the absolute *slop*—"

"Hey." Bev pursed her lips.

"Come now, Bev, it wasn't your best. Not by a long shot." Etheldra sniffed. "Barley soup. In the spring! Can't even imagine."

"I'm so sorry I offended your delicate sensibilities," Bev said with a chuckle. "I promise I'll never do it again."

"You never did tell us what was keeping you away from the inn," Bardoff said. "Another mystery?"

"You could say that," Bev said. "Seems like it was resolved without me, though. Happy that my part in the play is over, and I can get back to working here. Don't want the ghost of Wim McKee coming back to berate me for letting his beloved inn fall into disrepair."

That earned a chuckle from everyone, including the newcomer, who was still shoveling food into his mouth as if he hadn't eaten in years.

"What is it you're doing in town, Harold?" Earl asked. "Do you have a trade?"

"I used to," he said. "Found myself on the other side of a spat recently. But I'm an apothecary by trade."

Bev started, her head snapping to him as he pulled out a vial—and a single, yellow feather with it.

"G-Gerry?" Bev sputtered. "Is that you?"

The blood drained from his face as he looked Bev in the eyes. Bev couldn't believe she *hadn't* noticed it before. The turn of his mouth, the way he walked. Even the way his fingers spread out as he ate, like they were used to being *feathered*. Not to mention his voice, which had shifted slightly now that it was coming out of a human-sized throat.

"Gerry?" Etheldra scrutinized him. "Gerry Rickshaw? As I live and breathe."

"Rickshaw?" Earl frowned. "Wait, Bernard's brother?"

"Bernard has a brother?" Bardoff asked.

"Yes, Bernard has a brother," Gerry snapped. "Not surprised he never spoke of me, considering how jealous he was of my talents. And today! Practically threw me out of his shop when I walked in the front door. How do you like that?"

"How are you..." Bev began, but then thought better of it. Perhaps best not to ask where all his feathers had gone in front of the regulars. Etheldra might not think twice about it, but Bardoff and Earl would be a different story.

"Ten years since we've seen one another, and he treats me like that. Surely, he can't imagine what *I've* been through. Couldn't even offer me a bed or a kind word. Just told me to keep walking!"

On and on, he ranted, getting a sympathetic nod from Bardoff, and skeptical looks from Etheldra and Earl. Bev listened with an ear to find out what had happened after he'd been arrested, and how he'd managed to get the spell undone. But all he complained about were slights from before his stint in Lower Pigsend from his brother.

"And on that note," Etheldra said, rising as soon as there was a break in the ranting, "I've got to get going."

"Same." Earl followed her, depositing his bowl with Bev. "Glad to have you back, Bev."

Bev gave him a tight smile. "Me, too."

Bardoff was the last to leave, as he was caught in Gerry's restarted ranting, but eventually he, too, was able to excuse himself. Then it was just Gerry and Bev, and the silence of knowing each other's secrets.

"So," Bev started slowly, "you look different."

Gerry rolled his eyes. "Hmph."

"Care to share what happened?" Bev asked.

"Don't see how it's any of your business," he replied.

"It's not. But... Well, I'm sure you're happy to

be human again. Especially considering..." Bev didn't really know how to phrase 'you stole the protective talisman from the underground town' without offending him. She sincerely doubted Shamus had been kind enough to actually *give* him what he wanted, so maybe he'd managed to find the ingredients that had eluded him down below and done it himself.

"Yes." He shook himself like he was ruffling his feathers. "Well, I suppose I'll be starting fresh. I'd hoped for a better reunion with my brother, but it is what it is."

"I know that was probably disappointing," Bev said, trying for diplomacy. "Why didn't you say anything when you got here?"

"Was a bit surprised you didn't recognize me," he said. "Why didn't you tell your other diners where you've been?"

"Oh, I would've thought that was obvious," Bev said with a chuckle. "We get queen's soldiers in town every so often. I would hate one of them to find out about Lower Pigsend, especially with Percival looking so..." She searched for the right words. "Well, I suppose Shamus will have to figure something out now that you're no longer living there."

"Oh, I'm sure there's a great many things he's going to come to regret," Gerry said with a sly look. "I suppose I'd better get to bed. Long journey tomorrow."

"Where are you going next?"

He sighed. "South, probably. Would be nice to spend time in the sun for a change."

"Well, good night," Bev said. "Allen, the baker next door, will bring muffins in the morning. They aren't quite as amazing as Lillie's—"

"I'm sure they'll be a marked improvement from the magic-laced food I've been forced to eat all this time." Again, he ruffled his no-longer-there feathers. "Anyway. To bed."

He marched up the stairs, but Bev couldn't help herself.

"Gerry," she said. "Why did you take the talisman? To change yourself back?"

"That's my business," he replied with a quirked brow.

And with that, he continued up to his room and slammed the door.

"Ida was right. That was quite anticlimactic." Bev looked down at Biscuit, who wagged his tail. "What do we think, Biscuit?"

Biscuit watched her, wordlessly as ever.

"Suppose you're right," Bev said. "Not our puzzle to figure out. The talisman is back, the town is safe. Everything is—"

The door burst open, and PJ came running in, clutching his chest.

"PJ, what's wrong?" Bev said. "Are you all right?

You aren't about to transform, are you?"

"No, nothing like that." He took a deep breath. "I just...ran here. Wanted to tell...you straight away."

"What is it?" Bev asked.

"I've spent the day at the miller's," he said, straightening but still heaving deep breaths. "I wanted to see if anyone strange came by. Well, no one did, all day, until just now. Someone came out of *nowhere* and met with the miller. Gotta be the magical guy you were looking for."

"Really?" Bev chewed her lip. She'd just gone through the trouble of telling herself that Lower Pigsend's problems were theirs, and she had her hands full at the inn. But she couldn't leave this particular thread unraveled.

"Yeah," PJ said. "He's there now. But I don't know how long—"

"Good job, PJ," Bev said, looking at Biscuit. "C'mon. If we hurry, we may be able to catch him."

Chapter Twenty

As soon as he and Bev left the inn, Biscuit's tail perked up and his nose fell to the ground. Something magical was definitely in the air.

Bev had sent PJ home, as it was late and she didn't want him to get in trouble with his parents. At least, that was what she'd told him. In truth, she wasn't sure what kind of mischief she was about to uncover, and she didn't want the young dragon shifter anywhere near it.

The mill wheel was visible in the moonlight, but there weren't any lights burning. Bev held out hope that they hadn't lost the trail because Biscuit was still moving at a good clip, but she wasn't exactly sure what was going on.

As they drew closer, Bev slowed, keeping her ears out for any sound other than Biscuit's quiet footfalls. She didn't hear Sonny, or even the nicker of his horse in his stable—but she did hear voices.

"This isn't enough."

"Well, it's what I could find. Take it or leave it."

The first voice Bev recognized with a thrill of excitement. That was Shamus, who most certainly shouldn't have been on this side of things. The second was also somewhat familiar, but Bev couldn't quite place him. She peered over the fence, and caught a glimpse of three figures standing in the distance.

"We've got enough to contend with after this talisman debacle," Shamus said. "We need to give Percival a break. A real one, not just sneaking in a bag of nuts here and there."

"I'm one man, and I ain't got any magic, so you get what you get. If you'd like to source your own material, you are welcome to wander the countryside and make the deals."

"That's what we pay you for." His voice identified the third figure as Nog, though Bev should've recognized his short stature and knobby head.

"And the price is going up. I can't tell you how many soldiers I've run into in the past three months. It's as if they can *smell* the magic on me, you know? Takes all my wits just to keep them off my tail."

"We can't pay you more than we have," Shamus said. "But you don't understand, the people of Lower Pigsend… They need these things to survive. And Percival can't keep up."

"Then perhaps you should *enlighten* them as to the truth of their predicament."

"Are you joking?" Nog let out a loud snort. "They about lost their minds when they heard the talisman was gone. I busted my butt last week acting like I was looking for it just to keep them from rioting."

Bev swallowed. Did that mean…?

"So I guess it still hasn't been found?" The unknown man drawled.

"It's close," Shamus said. "The spell would've broken immediately had it been removed from the town. That it's still limping along is…well, it's a good sign. It's still in the town somewhere. We just need to *find* it."

"You're not still harassing that moleman, are you? Or the innkeeper?"

"We should be!" Nog barked. "Giant loophole in our protections, isn't it? All you have to do is stand on one side of the moleman's living room and toss the talisman across the barrier. Then it's all over."

Bev started. *What?*

"Seems rather a large oversight," the merchant drawled. "Maybe you should fix that."

"We've had *quite* a lot on our plate, keeping everyone fed and clothed," Shamus said with a dirty look. "But now that the people are happy with the talisman, and the innkeeper isn't coming to town anymore, we can fix the tunnel and the loopholes that have been discovered."

Bev's chest seized.

"Strange the wizard left that sort of thing up to chance?" the merchant asked.

"I honestly don't know how he set it up originally," Shamus said. "His mind works in mysterious ways I don't understand, and the spell he cast is far too complex for my level. But I have to assume he had a good reason for it."

"Not as if we can ask him to do anything, the loon," Nog chirped.

"But I do know he was clear: the queen's people can't walk past the spell," Shamus said. "And as long as that part of the spell remains intact, we're safe. Besides that, I think the innkeeper understands our predicament and will use discretion. I doubt she's walking around town, telling people about our existence."

Bev had to smile at his assessment of her.

"Back to the matter at hand," Shamus said. "I've bought Percival some time by telling the masses he needed a few days to rest after recasting the spell. I've told people to submit lists of things they need instead of queuing up." He pulled out a large stack of papers. "This is just from this afternoon."

The merchant gave it a sideways glance but said nothing.

"We're hoping if we can have him rest a few days, maybe even a week, we'll be able to get him coherent enough to modify the spell," Shamus said. "Which means we need *you* to get this stuff for us. All of it. Or else people are going to start asking questions."

"There's no way I can acquire all that without being noticed," the mystery man said, eyeing the stack of papers. "Whatever's the hardest for Percival to amplify, I'll—" He paused, turning quickly. "What was that?"

Bev's heart sank as Biscuit's white-tipped tail appeared in the clearing where the three men stood.

"That's… It's a dog," Shamus said.

"Not just any dog," Nog growled, turning to look. "Belongs to that innkeeper." He stomped forward, past Biscuit. "Well? Are you around here somewhere?" he called out into the night.

Bev realized she'd probably get more information if she just spoke with them, so she put her hands to her mouth. "Biscuit? Where'd you go?" She rose from her hiding spot, pretending she hadn't overheard the entire conversation. "Biscuit? I — Oh. Is that…? Officer Nog? Shamus? What in the world are you doing up here?"

"None of your business," Nog snapped. "Now

get back to your inn, before I—"

"Before you what?" Bev asked, coming to stand next to the three of them. She finally got a good look at the third man and recognition snapped in her mind. "You're the one who bought the tanddaes from Bathilda!"

He started. "Who are you?"

"Bev," she said, turning to cast an angry eye at Shamus and, more specifically, Nog. "You knew all along, didn't you?"

Nog snorted. "Don't know what you're talking about."

"Oh, come now. It's quite obvious." Bev put her hands on her hip. "You knew exactly what I was talking about when I told you someone up here had sold a herd of tanddaes to someone in Lower Pigsend. And now you're here, buying barley from Sonny and selling it to Lonny. Among other things, I'd wager." She decided to forego her ruse of ignorance. "I overheard everything. You've had this tunnel open all along and kept everyone in Lower Pigsend in the dark. Why did you send me on a wild goose chase if you're the ones smuggling—"

"Ain't no smuggling about it," Nog barked.

"Fine, *bringing* goods to and from town?" Bev asked. "Surely, it would've been simpler to have just left me and Merv alone?"

Shamus and Nog shared a look, but Shamus was the one to speak first. "We *did* intend to leave you alone, once we'd figured out you hadn't taken the talisman. I can't imagine *why* Officer Nog insisted you tell him the information we already knew."

"Because I wanted to make sure Winston was the only one with a tunnel," Nog snapped at Shamus.

"Of course he's the only one with a tunnel," Shamus snapped. "Because *I'm* the one making them."

"Could've been another loophole like that moleman's living room!" Nog shot back. "I thought she'd get me a name and that'd be that. Next thing I know, she's walking all over town, mucking things up for all of us, asking questions we don't want asked and making things difficult."

"Because you threatened my friend Merv when he'd done nothing wrong," Bev said. "There's no way I could ignore that."

"I wasn't *threatening* him. I was *testing* the spell to make sure it was still there," Nog said. "As I said."

"And I'm sure you were quite pleasant about the whole ordeal," Bev said with a glare. "Look, if it was such a problem, why not just tell me the truth?"

"Because the talisman is still in the town," Shamus said. "And the *last* thing we wanted was for the thief to realize what it would take to break the spell. We're still holding out hope we can find the talisman before it's too late."

"Then why the whole fuss with Gerry?" Bev asked. "Who, by the way, showed up human at my inn this after..." She blinked in realization. "You did that, didn't you? He wasn't guilty at all. It was a bribe so he'd take the blame and quell the concern in town."

"We needed the people to think all was well," Shamus said quietly. "They were starting to panic." He shook his head. "Can you imagine? All those people? It would be a calamity. So in the interest of their safety, Gerry agreed to take the blame and leave."

"And you gave him something for his trouble," Bev said with a look. "Turning him human. Why hadn't you done that before?"

"Magic is a finite resource," Shamus said. "How could we possibly focus on turning one wayward apothecary back to human when we had to make sure the town was fed, clothed, and had adequate supplies?"

"So this tunnel," Bev said, nodding to the hole behind them. "Is it exempt from the spell?"

"I create a doorway," Shamus said. "Temporarily allows us passage. But I'm the only one who can open and close it, and I stand right here to make sure nothing goes through that I don't know about."

"And it's only things you can sneak into the town?" Bev asked. "You can't tell the people that Percival can suddenly make a bag of flour?"

Shamus shook his head. "We had two years of very clear rules around magic. Had a lot of consternation in the community about why they couldn't have this, or how we couldn't do a thing when their bags of flour and fruit ran out. If we started changing things, there would be questions, and questions lead to...well, more questions that we're not keen to answer. So we do what we can, helping with the goods we know Percival had magically replicated in the past."

"And the barley?" Bev asked with a quirked brow.

"*Nog* can explain that one," Shamus said with pursed lips. "As it wasn't my idea."

"I like real beer," the goblin said. "Suffered through two years of the magical stuff 'fore we started bringing in real supplies from up here. Lonny and I have an agreement that he'll keep it quiet, and he was able to sneak in some better beer to make us all happy."

Bev did some quick math in her head. "So you've been helping Percival for what? Three years? And he still looks that rough?"

"He looked worse before we stepped in," Shamus said. "He still does most of the replication that you see, but where we can feed in the real stuff, we do."

Bev glared at Nog. "And the magistrate? I can only assume I was right in believing he's a fabrication."

"When some noticed the fresher ingredients, they began to ask questions," Shamus said. "So Officers Bola and Nog were put on the case to make it look like the magistrate was keeping everything in order."

"When in fact, they were the ones bringing in the outside goods," Bev said.

"For the sake of the wizard," Shamus said. "The more we can take off his plate, the better."

"You said the talisman is still in town," Bev asked. "Why haven't you been able to use that magical scanner thing you used at the inn to locate it?"

"It only works when there's no other magic around," Shamus said. "There's too much interference in Lower Pigsend. We aren't even close to finding it. Whoever took it hid it well."

"Is that why you haven't bothered to do anything about Merv's tunnel?" Bev asked. "Leaving it open like that?"

"We've had too many *other* things on our plate to mess with him," Nog said.

"Especially since the magic that kept us safe is still, theoretically, keeping us safe," Shamus said. "But if whoever took the talisman is somehow able to get it beyond the boundaries of the town, the spell will break." He paused. "We have no choice but to close the tunnel."

Bev chewed her lip. "I do hate that idea, but it's better that Lower Pigsend be safe. I'll surely miss Merv—"

"We would be closing Merv off from Lower Pigsend," Shamus said. "He can still come up to your world as he sees fit, but he won't be allowed to set foot in our town ever again."

"How are you going to accomplish that?" Bev asked. "He can just dig another tunnel—"

"He was exempt from the first spell because we hadn't accounted for topsiders," Shamus said. "But while I can't adjust the parameters for an entire population of people who live up here, I can adjust it for one person—er, moleman."

"But if you find the talisman," Bev said slowly, "you won't have to do that, right?"

"We may just do it anyway," Nog snapped. "Too dangerous to have people knowing about Lower Pigsend to leave the door wide open like that."

Bev glanced at the merchant, who'd been awfully quiet during this exchange. He'd *specifically* mentioned Lower Pigsend to Bathilda. It was the only reason she'd known to ask Merv about the place.

"How many people have you told about Lower Pigsend?" Bev asked, and he pursed his lips. "It seems to me all this sneaking around is wholly unnecessary. People will understand, I think, that there's a need to bring new items in. That the town can't rely on one wizard alone to keep them going. And if Merv's tunnel being open all this time—and a queen's soldier even coming to his house—"

The three men started. "What?" Shamus gasped. "When?"

"Ages ago," Bev said with a wave of her hand. "I didn't *realize* he was a queen's soldier, as he was hiding his identity from me. But I brought him to Merv's home for a quick chat. And he hadn't been the wiser about the town that existed just beyond his front door."

"We've got to close his tunnel for sure, now," Nog said. "Queen's people have been near enough."

"Now hold on," Bev said, fearing she might've said too much. "Look, why don't we think about this for a moment. About who might've taken the talisman."

"What do you think we've been doing?" Nog snapped.

"It was taken the day I arrived in town," Bev continued, ignoring him. "Which means the person who stole it must've been prompted by something that day."

"Obviously, your arrival," Shamus said.

"Maybe, but it might not be that simple," Bev said. "So if I'm the culprit, I take the talisman, and I run it up Merv's tunnel, but before I can make it to Merv's door, I'm stopped by the barrier spell." She ran her hands through her hair, thinking through the scenario. "Merv didn't see anyone strange that day, but—"

She stopped.

"I know who took the talisman. And I have a feeling they're going to be trying to break the spell, if they haven't already."

Chapter Twenty~One

With Shamus and Nog behind her, and Biscuit at her heels, Bev hurried along the well-worn path from Pigsend to Merv's house. She prayed she was wrong, that she'd seen everything all wrong, and when she reached Merv's house, there would be some other perpetrator waiting there. But the evidence was too clear to ignore, so much so that Bev was kicking herself for not seeing it before.

"Where are we going?" Shamus asked. "Wouldn't it be faster to go back down through the tunnel?"

"Unless the culprit already broke the spell," Bev said, leading them through the dark farmland.

"I would know," Shamus said,

"Would you?" Nog asked with a quirked brow. "You all-powerful apprentice."

"Shut it, goblin."

"Both of you quit bickering," Bev said, running into the tunnel. It was darker than usual, and without her glowing stick, which she'd left behind in her haste to get out the door, Bev could barely keep her footing. But after walking this path so many days in a row, she almost had it memorized.

Merv's door appeared ahead, and the lights were on.

Bev rapped on the door. "Merv?"

No answer.

"Merv, are you there?"

"Who do you think it is?" Shamus asked.

Bev winced as she tried to open the door, and it wouldn't budge. She rammed it with her shoulder once, but only produced a sore shoulder.

"Let me," Shamus said, pulling out his wand. With a flourish, the door unlocked and swung open.

"Wish you'd done that before I'd broken my shoulder," Bev muttered, but walked inside. The sound of Merv's snoring echoed through the space, and standing in the living room was...

"Lillie?" Shamus gasped.

Her eyes had widened as the trio burst through the door, and she licked her lips nervously, holding the pail.

"Lillie, how could you?" Bev asked, breaking the

silence. "*You* stole the talisman? Why would you do such a thing?"

"You don't know what it's like down there," she said, her voice rising an octave. "Never seeing the sun, never getting real food. A pobyd who can't use flour? It's against my very nature to sell the things I was selling." She shook her head. "All because *they* can't stop lying to save their own skins."

"The lies we tell are for the greater good," Shamus said. "If we started bringing crates of goods into Lower Pigsend—"

"What? People would know they've been bamboozled?" Lillie snapped. "You'd have to answer for the past three years? Lying to us about bringing in fresh ingredients, as if I, a pobyd, couldn't tell the difference." She swallowed. "So when Bev arrived, talking about a herd of tanddaes that had been sold, I thought the spell had been broken. When I realized it hadn't, I spread pepper all over the Merchant's House and took the talisman to break the spell."

"The sneezing," Bev said.

"Where have you been keeping it?" Shamus asked.

She gestured to the house. "Right here in Merv's house, so when the spell broke, I could just carry it across with me. But after a few days, it didn't— didn't even seem like it was waning. The door Bev walked through was still invisible to me. Then Nog said it was still inside the city, and I realized that the talisman needed to actually *cross* the barrier to no longer work." She gestured to Merv, who was still snoring in his chair. "I tried for days to get it across."

"That's why you laced Merv's cookies with too much calming potion," Bev said, her opinion of Lillie dropping with every confession.

"Not enough to hurt him," Lillie said, glancing at Merv with a hint of concern. "Just so he wouldn't wake while I tried to break the spell. But it became clear to me that I needed someone else to take the talisman across. I knew you'd never do it, Bev, and then..." She lifted a shoulder. "The opportunity presented itself."

As if on cue, the door behind Bev and the others opened, and Gerry walked in, looking smug and victorious—at least until he noticed Shamus and Nog glaring at him.

"W-well, hello, friends," he said, nervously. "What are you doing here?"

"Stopping you from breaking the spell," Shamus said, pulling out his wand and pointing it at Lillie. "Don't you dare."

She huffed and stayed her hand.

"And here I thought you'd become chivalrous in your feathered old age," Nog snarled at Gerry. "Offering to take the blame so the city would be safe."

"Hardly," Gerry scoffed.

"What was in it for you?" Bev asked Gerry. "You had your freedom. Why did you need to come back here—"

"Because of *him*," Gerry said, pointing at Shamus, who was speechless as he stared at the two of them. "All his *lies*. Goodness knows I gave everything I had, all of my best potions and ingredients, and he *never* held up his end of the bargain."

"Are you still a chicken?" Shamus snapped. "No? I'd say you're doing all right. And you got to leave Lower Pigsend, too. There's no need to endanger the lives of everyone in town just to get back at me."

"As it stands," he said lightly. "I'm not the one in charge of breaking it. I'm just here to catch it."

"Lillie," Bev said, still eyeing the talisman in her hand, "you don't have to do this, you know. Shamus can modify the spell. He can let you out."

She hesitated, but Gerry stepped forward.

"If he could, he would have," he said. "We all know Shamus doesn't have the sort of power he claims to. Led me on for three years!" He opened his hands. "Come now, hand over the talisman."

"Lillie, you're a pobyd," Shamus said. "The queen doesn't like your kind, remember? That's why you ended up down in Lower Pigsend in the first place."

"There's a pobyd in Bev's village," Lillie said,

pointing at her. "She told me so."

"Not a real one, and Allen doesn't have any magic," Bev said. "Fernley's was so scant it barely registered. You're really much safer in Lower Pigsend."

"Or," Gerry drawled, "I'm sure there's a queen's soldier in town who'd be happy to take it off your hands in exchange for a full pardon."

All three Lower Pigsend citizens gasped in horror.

"I would *never*..." Lillie began, but Shamus cut her off.

"If you go through with this, you're effectively leaving everyone open to the queen's people," he said.

"You could turn around," Bev added, "go back to your bakery—"

"And live the rest of my life in the dark?" She shook her head. "No, I've come this far. It's time to finish what I started." She planted her feet, and swung the pail in her hands, readying it to throw. "Ready, Gerry? Catch."

She tossed the talisman into the air, and Bev held her breath as it flew toward Gerry. But before it landed in his hands, it stopped.

Lillie blinked. "What the—"

The talisman zoomed backward, landing in the wizened hands of...

"Percival?" Shamus took a step back, his hand

coming to his chest.

Bev could scarcely believe her eyes. The old, decrepit wizard had suddenly rebounded, and while still white-haired and wizened, he was spry, bright-eyed, and had filled out to a healthier-looking size. His robes no longer sagged on his shoulders, instead swishing around as he stepped into the room, his pointed hat scraping the ceiling.

Biscuit popped up from his spot by Bev's feet and wagged his tail wildly, as if Percival was the most delicious piece of rare steak that had just walked into the room.

"I'll take this." Even Percival's voice was stronger, like he'd de-aged twenty years. "No use breaking a perfectly fine spell."

"W-what happened to you?" Lillie gasped, taking a step back.

"Turns out a few days' rest can do wonders for the soul," Percival said. "Now that I'm back in my right mind, I've got a few things to say." He turned to Shamus and Nog. "First, what in the *world* have you two been doing? A magistrate? Scaring the people half to death with threats and lies and shadows?" He shook his head. "You know better than that, apprentice."

"We did our best under the circumstances," Shamus said, but his face dropped.

"Did you?" He scoffed, turning to Gerry. "And you—your lousy tinctures only did the bare minimum, so I suppose it's no surprise that you wanted to escape to foist your lackluster talents on everyone else."

Gerry made a face.

"And what is this poor attempt at a cloaking spell?" Percival asked, snapping his wand in the air.

With a loud *pop*, the man once again became a yellow-feathered chicken.

Gerry gasped in horror, looking at the wings where his hands had just been and stared at Percival as if he'd completely lost his mind. "What'd you do that for? I just got rid of these feathers!"

"I simply undid the very *basic* spell my apprentice cast on you," Percival said with a glare at Shamus. "It was due to expire in a week, anyway. Bit of a nasty surprise, Shamus. You know better than to cast such flimsy magic."

The apprentice again ducked his head.

"Serves you right," Bev said to Gerry.

"Because it seems you only had an ancillary hand in this debacle," Percival continued, "I will give you your choice. You may return to your apothecary in Lower Pigsend, having to answer for your perceived guilt and tarnished reputation. Or you can walk the surface world."

Gerry shook his feathers, loosening a few of them. "What about this?"

"What about it?" Percival quirked a brow. "If I were you, I'd opt for the world where you aren't looked at twice. But make your choice now, because where you stand in the next few moments is where you'll be."

Percival's wand tip glowed, and Gerry hightailed it toward the door to Lower Pigsend, leaving a few yellow feathers in his wake.

"Now as for you," Percival said, turning on Lillie. The pobyd took a step back, her eyes growing wider as she cowered. "What would be an apt punishment for you?"

"Don't turn me into a chicken," she whispered.

"No. I think in this case, giving you what you want is punishment enough," Percival said. He pulled out his wand and waved it around, a shimmering trail of magic falling behind him.

Lillie winced, waiting for the blow, but nothing happened. "W-what did you do?"

"I modified the talisman's spell," he said. "Everyone in Lower Pigsend in. Everyone in the queen's service—and Lillie the pobyd—out."

"Out?" She squeaked. For someone who'd gone through a lot of trouble to escape Lower Pigsend, being faced with the reality of it seemed to terrify her.

"Out. It's what you wanted, after all." Percival turned to Shamus. "Come, apprentice. We have much to discuss about the past few years. And Officer Nog, too." He paused, nodding to Bev. "Thank you for your part in this. It's nice to know there are still good people in the upper world willing to help."

"Of course," Bev said. "You've certainly made quite the recovery in such a short time."

"A story for a later time." He winked. "Come, Shamus, Nog."

And with that, the trio walked through the door.

For a few minutes, the only sound was Merv's snoring and the occasional snort as he started then fell back asleep. Biscuit sat at Bev's feet, his gaze on Bev. Bev's gaze was on Lillie, waiting for her to make the next move. And Lillie's gaze was fixed on the door to Lower Pigsend. After shaking herself, she walked toward the door and stared at it.

"The door's gone," she said, matter-of-factly as she ran her hand over it. "All I see is Merv's wall."

"Well, that's probably for the best," Bev said. "Considering you aren't allowed down there anymore."

The pobyd's shoulders slumped, and as she slowly turned, there was angst, regret, and sadness on her face. Not to mention a tinge of fear that perhaps should've been there all along to keep her from making such an awful mistake.

"What am I supposed to do now?" Lillie whispered.

"I daresay do what you wanted," Bev said, more than a little annoyance in her voice. "Go off and enjoy your life in the sun. Bake with *real flour.*

Whatever else you envisioned when you decided to steal something so precious to so many people."

Lillie chewed her lip. "Bev, I know you don't understand, but—"

"I think I understand quite well," Bev said. "What you did was selfish. Not only to the people of Lower Pigsend, but to dear, sweet Merv."

She lowered her gaze, and Bev felt like a teacher chastising a misbehaving pupil.

"I just couldn't stand being down there any longer," Lillie whispered. "I know it was wrong, but I just couldn't take another day."

"You endangered everyone in town," Bev said.

"I thought..." She swallowed. "I thought Percival could just cast a new one once I was clear. I didn't..." She met Bev's gaze. "Bev, I would *never* do what Gerry said. Give up the talisman for a pardon from the queen. Who's to say they'd even give me one?" She shook her head. "I really just thought... Well, there's no use in rehashing it now. What's done is done."

Biscuit rose from his spot and trotted over to Lillie, sitting down next to her and looking up with his large, golden eyes. Lillie made no move to pet him, but Biscuit nuzzled her calf. At first, Bev glared at him for offering comfort to someone who'd hurt (or potentially hurt) so many people, but as she watched Lillie stand there, her gaze growing distant, a small part of Bev could understand her desperation, even if she couldn't excuse the methods.

"I suppose I'd better get to it," Lillie said, swallowing. She picked up one of Merv's blankets and tucked it under her arm as if it were a precious gift. "Should take one, as this might be the last time I'll get to see him."

"Where are you going?" Bev asked as she followed the pobyd up the tunnel.

"I'm sure I don't have any family left in Sheepsburg," she said. "The queen's people probably made sure of that." She shrugged. "I'll make my way. Just can't wait to see the sun."

Bev could practically feel the dejection when the pobyd realized it was the middle of the night.

"Suppose it serves me right that I can't even see the stars," she said with a shiver as she gazed up at the cloudy sky. "I forgot how cold it can be. Don't suppose you know of a warm rock I can sleep on, do you?"

Biscuit let out a low whine and nudged Bev. She glared down at her laelaps, offended he'd even suggest what she assumed he was suggesting. But as Lillie left the tunnel, wrapping herself in Merv's blanket but still shivering in the cold, spring night, Bev let out a frustrated sigh.

"Fine. Come on, then." She really was too nice for her own good. "Let's get you set up at the inn."

"W-what?" Lillie's eyes went wide again. "What

do you mean?"

"I mean that as horrible as you are, nobody deserves to sleep without a roof over their head," Bev said. "You can stay at the inn tonight."

"Bev, that's so—"

"But in payment, you're going to help the baker next door," Bev said. "He was just telling me this morning he's got a bit too much on his plate."

Lillie nodded emphatically. "Bev, you're… Thank you."

"It's more than you deserve," Bev snapped. "This is the *only* second chance you'll get from me, understand? And if you do anything to hurt my friends or family in Pigsend, you'll regret it. I may not be able to turn you into a half-chicken, but—"

"I promise," she said, with a forlorn look back toward the tunnel. "I do regret mixing Merv up in all this. He's been such a good friend." She swallowed, her gaze back on Bev. "You aren't going to…tell him, are you?"

Bev pursed her lips. "No. Only because it would hurt his gentle heart too much to know how you've betrayed him. But I *do* expect you to make it up to him, you hear me? Lots of baked goods and don't let me catch you putting a drop of anything funny in them."

She nodded.

"Well, come on," Bev said.

But Lillie stayed where she was. "There isn't…a

soldier staying at the inn, is there?"

"Bit late to be worrying about that now, isn't it?" Bev said before softening. "But no. It's just a trio of travelers. You're safe for tonight."

Chapter Twenty~Two

"Wow."

Bev spun around, mid-pump, as Lillie's voice carried through the yard. The pobyd's large, round eyes were fixed to the east, where the sun was coming up over the horizon. The sky was a vivid pink and orange, with high clouds streaking across it.

"You're up early," Bev said, returning to her work.

"I haven't seen the sun in five years. I'm certainly not going to miss a moment of it." She crossed the yard to take the bucket from her. "Let me help."

Bev told her where to take the water, and Sin

brayed loudly at the intruder. Lillie patted her on the nose to calm her and gave her some carrots. The mule quieted instantly, and Bev wondered how much of Lillie's pobyd magic extended to the ingredients before they were baked.

"What's next?" Lillie asked.

"Well, I've got to get to my bread," Bev said, as she hadn't had a chance to make it the night before. "And Allen should be by soon with his muffins."

"Made with real flour?" Lillie clapped her hands. "I can't wait. May I help with your baking?"

Bev tried to hide the grimace. "I don't... Um. The rosemary bread is a source of pride. And—"

"And you don't want my magic getting in the way," she said with a nod. "Understood."

"Maybe you could sweep the front room for me," Bev offered.

"Be happy to."

Lillie seemed adequately chastened by her new circumstances, sweeping and dusting and cleaning without a peep out of her.

At seven on the dot, Allen walked in, but stopped short when his gaze landed on Lillie. "Oh. Good morning. Erm. Are you a guest?"

"Morning, Allen," Bev said, walking out to greet him and wiping dough off her hands. "This is Lillie."

"Lillie." He did a double-take. "Lillie-Lillie? Lillie from..." He pointed down.

She nodded, her cheeks turning red.

"What are you doing up here?" Allen asked.

Bev could've told Allen that Lillie was the culprit, that she'd caused all sorts of problems down below, and she was here because Bev felt too bad to leave her out in the cold.

But she couldn't.

Of course, Bev was still furious with the pobyd, not only for the disruption to her own life, the danger she'd posed to Lower Pigsend, and all the angst she'd caused Merv. As horrible as that was, she was also a victim of the circumstances. Of the queen's machinations and the need to hide her magic. Should the wrong soldier come into town, she'd see the consequences of her actions soon enough.

"Lillie was able to get the wizard to release her from the spell keeping her in Lower Pigsend," Bev said, after a moment. "Apparently she missed flour a little too much."

Lillie seemed just as surprised as Bev that she hadn't been ratted out. "Y-yes. That's right."

"Flour?" Allen thought for a moment. "Oh, that's right. You had to bake with nuts, right?"

"Nut flour," she said, nodding to the basket in his hands. "Are those..." She inhaled. "They smell divine."

"I'm sure they're nothing compared to yours, but..." He offered her one. "Be honored if you tried one."

She didn't need to be told twice, diving into the basket and stuffing one into her mouth in one movement. Her eyes widened as she savored the flavor, and a single tear fell down her cheek.

"This is..." She muttered, closing her eyes and shaking her head. "This is the most delicious thing I've ever had in my life."

"You're joking," Allen said with a nervous laugh. "It's just a blueberry muffin."

"You don't understand," she whispered. "I haven't had a real blueberry or real sugar or *flour* in five years. It's incredible. You're incredible."

Allen's face turned the color of a tomato. "Well, um. Better be getting the rest of the batch over to Etheldra's."

"Before you go," Bev said, "I know you're busy these next few months, so if you need an extra set of hands in the kitchen, Lillie would be happy to help you today."

"Really?" Another nervous laugh. "I...Sure. I could use the help."

"And maybe..." Lillie said, her voice quiet and meek. "You could help me figure out how to hide my magic?"

"Right. That I can probably do." He turned to Lillie. "I get started pretty early, though."

"What baker doesn't?" Lillie shrugged. "Is four too early?"

"A bit. I get going around five," he said.

"Then I'll see you tomorrow morning around five." She brightened, giving perhaps the most genuine smile Bev had seen from her. "Thank you. I'm excited to work with you."

"R-right." He took a step back, his cheeks still flushed. "See you around, Bev!"

And with that, he dashed out the door.

"My, he's certainly sweet," Lillie said, watching the door with more than a little interest.

"He's getting married in a few months," Bev said, eyeing her. "So don't get any ideas."

"Oh." She jumped. "Of course. Wouldn't dream of it."

~

Lillie showed up bright and early at Allen's, and Bev had to admit that the muffins that came out were head and shoulders above what Allen put out. Allen had nothing but praises for her and actually thanked Bev for connecting them. Lillie, too, seemed comfortable working alongside him, and was dutiful in handing over her gold coin to stay and eat at the inn every night.

It was almost a week later before Bev finally drummed up the courage to return to Merv's, unsure what she was going to say. Before she left, she asked Lillie if she wanted to go with her.

"I don't think that's wise," Lillie said with a sigh. "But I do have a letter you can deliver. It's a full confession and apology."

"Really?" Bev took the letter from her. "I thought you didn't want him to know what you'd done."

"He deserves the truth," she said. "And if, after knowing what I've done, he still wants to be my friend, then I'd be delighted." She paused, thinking. "But maybe I could sweeten the deal with a box of cookies."

"Just make sure to leave out the calming draught," Bev said.

Lillie's face went pink.

~

The next morning, Bev gathered the box of cookies, Lillie's letter, and her walking shoes and trekked the long walk to her friend's house. It seemed almost *longer* than ever, and she was happy that her daily trips were at an end.

Merv was happy to see her, and even happier to find out that Lillie had made at least a temporary home in Pigsend.

"Goodness, it all seems to be sorted now, doesn't it?" Merv said. "And I hear Lillie managed to make her escape. Can't imagine why she'd want to give up the safety of the town."

"Well, Lillie has an explanation for that," Bev said, reaching into the basket and handing over the letter. "I'll let you read it in private—"

But the moleman ripped it open and read it

before Bev could finish, and Bev's heart broke as his eyes lit up then fell, and his whole face drooped in sadness.

"I can't believe it," Merv whispered. "Lillie? How could she?"

"Desperation, I suppose," Bev said.

"And you've forgiven her?" Merv asked.

"I don't know about forgiven, but I couldn't let her fend for herself. She certainly seems remorseful, and she's been helpful across the street. As long as the people in Lower Pigsend are safe..."

He folded the letter, his voice wet. "I'll need a few days to think about this, but goodness... Lillie was such a dear friend." He picked up the large handkerchief and blew his nose. "I'm not sure I know what to think about all this."

Bev pulled out the cookies, wanting to wait until he knew the truth before handing them over. "She also sent these, by way of an apology. She promises there's nothing but lemon icing on them."

Merv opened the box and inhaled, his eyes growing wide. They were flour-based cookies, and based on the scent wafting from them, Lillie had used *all* her magic to make them delectable.

"Well..." Merv popped one into his mouth. "Maybe..." He chewed, a low groan coming from him. "Maybe I might be persuaded to forgive her... if she brings me more cookies. But I want a variation! I want chocolate. I want cinnamon. Fruit pies. Tiered cakes. Tarts. Muffins."

Bev had to laugh. "I'll be sure to pass on the message."

There was a knock on the other door, the one that led to Lower Pigsend. Merv beckoned them to come in, and Bev rose suddenly as a still-sprightly Percival walked in, his robes trailing him.

"Percival! Goodness, what in the world are you doing here?" Bev asked.

"I'd cast a notification spell on Merv's living room to let me know the next time you came," he said. "Hope you don't mind, Merv."

"Not at all," he said, rising. "Let me put on a pot of tea."

Percival sat on the couch. "I wanted to thank you again for all you did for the people of Lower Pigsend."

"I hope Shamus wasn't in too much trouble," Bev said. "Were you aware of what was going on?"

"Sometimes," he said. "I don't believe my apprentice set out to let it go as far as it did, and once the town became overly reliant on me, it seemed he couldn't stop the cart from rolling down the hill." He paused. "I did gather the townsfolk and let them know of that magistrate farce. It's not right to keep people in the dark like that."

"I quite agree," Bev said.

"Now that everyone knows we've been carting in goods from the surface, there's obviously a demand for *more* things. So we'll have to square that circle and find the best way to minimize our risk while ensuring our people get what they need."

"There's a twice-weekly farmers' market on the other side of Pigsend," Bev said. "They've just opened up for the warmer months again."

"Then I'll be sure to send Officer Nog to frequent it," he said.

"Not Winston?" Bev asked.

"We're indebted to him for his help," Percival said. "But understandably, the townsfolk weren't too pleased with the subterfuge these past few years. It might be good to find Officer Nog a useful task to ingratiate himself so he can show his face around town again. We'll set Mr. Winston to finding the larger items that are a bit trickier to find."

"So no more replication spells for you?" Bev asked hopefully.

"Unfortunately, that's still very much necessary," Percival said. "But as it stands, I've got full control of my faculties now, and I don't believe I'll be losing them again any time soon. And honestly, it's all thanks to you, Bev."

"Me?" She laughed. "I didn't do a thing."

"Oh, but you did." He reached under his shirt to tug a small chain, and pulled out...

"The amulet!" Bev exclaimed. "It's fixed!"

Indeed, the wooden piece that had been buried in Bev's garden was now mended, and seemed to enjoy its new status, glowing and shimmering as if it were alive.

"Steward brought it to me the other day," he said. "What with the townsfolk put on hold for a few days, I was able to get my head clear and speak with him. He showed me the talisman pieces, and I knew immediately what it was. I used a bit of magic to mend it, and it sprang right to life, restoring my own power."

"R-really?" Bev cleared her throat. "Is that what it does?"

"It's a wizard's aid," he said. "Meant to enhance a wizard's innate magic as they go about their business. Quite the fortuitous find, especially in my line of work." He chuckled, the absence of his wheezing more palpable than ever. "Wherever did you come across it?"

"Well, it was actually buried in my garden," Bev said, slowly. "And I think it might've been…mine?"

He furrowed his brow. "How do you mean?"

She explained her history, emphasizing she hadn't a clue who she was and, while she hadn't *shown* any signs of magic, she'd been given visions of her life before and her role in the great war.

Percival listened intently and nodded. "I know of a group of wizards who served the king directly. They were powerful, far more powerful than me. The queen was keen to get rid of them. But for obvious reasons, that was a difficult row to hoe." He smiled at her. "You said it was yours?"

Bev let out a bark halfway between a laugh and a scoff. "I'm not a powerful... I don't even have a lick of magic. Soldiers have been up and down this countryside, staying at my inn, and although they've been curious about me, they haven't ever demonstrated I'm anything more than a simple innkeeper."

"Perhaps you came across the talisman some other way," he said. "Er... Do you want it back? Steward said—"

She shook her head. "No, by all means. I think it's much more useful to you than to me. I'm happy to be rid of it."

"Well, I'd say that worked out well," Merv said, appearing in the doorway to the kitchen with a tray of tea and three large cups. "Tea?"

~

Bev had a lovely visit with Percival and Merv, although the wizard didn't offer any more specifics on the amulet. Instead, he spoke of his past, where he'd come from, and his vision for the town. Merv was a gracious host, pouring more tea than either of them could possibly drink, and before long, Bev noted the time and had to make her exit. She told Percival to call on her if ever Lower Pigsend needed anything—as long as it didn't require her to make daily trips again.

On the way back to town, she thought about the

talisman, and the power it seemed to give to Percival. She was, as she'd said, very happy to be rid of it and that it had restored his strength, but she couldn't help but wonder…what might it do if she were to wear it in its mended state?

And for that matter, what had she done in the past to warrant needing it in the first place?

For the answer to that question, Bev could look no farther than across the street.

With fluttering nerves, Bev knocked on the back door of the butcher shop, which was open to let the spring air in. Vellora was working on a hanging carcass but stopped and wiped her forehead with the back of her hand, smiling at Bev.

"Bev! What brings you back this way?" She thumbed toward the front room. "Ida's out there."

"I wanted to ask you something," Bev said, walking inside with her hands clenched together. Vellora had never taken questions about her time in the war well, and Bev didn't like kicking that hornet's nest. But Vellora might be the only one who knew. "About my past. And maybe…yours?"

As predicted, Vellora's eyes grew stormy. "Yeah?"

"I told you I was looking into it, just so I could be prepared in case someone like Dag Flanigan comes back to cause trouble," Bev said. "Fortune favors the prepared and all."

A curt nod as the butcher went back to carving. "Mm."

"I took the talisman to Lower Pigsend. Turns out it's a...wizard's aid sort of thing. Helps a magical user do magic, well, better, I suppose." She tilted her head, watching the ripples of Vellora's muscles as she worked. "Do you know anything about that?"

"Can't imagine why you'd think I would."

And here came the difficult part. "At the solstice, when you were telling me about your time in the army. That particular battle that was so awful." She winced as Vellora sliced through the meat with more force than was necessary. "I had a vision. I think I was there, too."

That caused Vellora to turn around. "What? You were?"

"I don't know for sure, but I think I was. I think I've met Dag Flanigan before, too," Bev said, starting to pace. "But I don't know for sure. I certainly don't have anything other than flashes of memories. And who knows if they're even mine? That amulet could've been tinged with something, and I just think I'm remembering when they're someone else's experience."

"Do you really think that or do you hope that?" Vellora asked slowly.

"Percival—the wizard down in Lower Pigsend— said he knew of a group of wizards who wore that amulet. Said they reported directly to the king. Powerful sort. Famous, too." Bev sucked in a breath.

"Which leads me to my question—"

"I don't know anything about that." It wasn't accusatory or defensive, just a statement. "I was a lowly foot soldier. Just enough to keep my own head on, not pay attention to what was going on with the spellcasters."

Bev nodded. "Well, I didn't mean to bother you with it. But I was hoping…"

She turned to leave, and was almost out the door when Vellora called to her, walking over with a nervous look on her face.

"I still sometimes send letters to my old commander," she said. "He might know something about it, if I asked him."

"I couldn't ask you to do something like that," Bev said. "Might get you in trouble with your registrar."

"Is it something you really want to keep uncovering?" Vellora asked. "If it is, I'll write the letter. But only if you're sure this is a road you want to walk down."

Bev once again twisted her hands over each other. "Well, I've come this far. Might as well keep going."

Bev continues her adventures in

Acknowlegments

As always, first thanks goes to my husband for believing in me and for managing the toddler in the evenings. Thanks, also, go to my son, for continuing to insist upon his six o'clock bedtime so I could write yet another book in the dark. Shout-out to Ms. Rachel, too. You're the real MVP.

Thanks to Chelsea, Danielle, and Lisa for being the all-star team who helps keep me going. And to my writer pals, Brett, Kelsey, and Emily, for keeping me sane.

Also By the Author

The Princess Vigilante Series

Brynna has been protecting her kingdom as a masked vigilante until one night, she's captured by the king's guards. Instead of arresting her, the captain tells her that her father and brother have been assassinated and she must hang up her mask and become queen.

The Princess Vigilante series is a four-book young adult epic fantasy series, perfect for fans of Throne of Glass and Graceling.

The Seod Croí Chronicles

After her father's murder, princess Ayla is set to take the throne — but to succeed, she needs the magical stone her evil stepmother stole. Fortunately, wizard apprentice Cade and knight Ward are both eager to win Ayla's favor.

A Quest of Blood and Stone is the first book in the *Seod Croí* chronicles and is available now in eBook, paperback, and hardcover.

Also By the Author

The Madion War Trilogy

He's a prince, she's a pilot, they're at war. But when they are marooned on a deserted island hundreds of miles from either nation, they must set aside their differences and work together if they want to survive.

The Madion War Trilogy is a fantasy romance available now in eBook, Paperback, and Hardcover.

empath

Lauren Dailey is in break-up hell, but if you ask her she's doing just great. She hears a mysterious voice promising an easy escape from her problems and finds herself in a brand new world where she has the power to feel what others are feeling. Just one problem—there's a dragon in the mountains that happens to eat Empaths. And it might be the source of the mysterious voice tempting her deeper into her own darkness.

Empath is a stand-alone fantasy that is available now in eBook, Paperback, and Hardcover.

About the Author

S. Usher Evans was born and raised in Pensacola, Florida. After a decade of fighting bureaucratic battles as an IT consultant in Washington, DC, she suffered a massive quarter-life-crisis. She found fighting dragons was more fun than writing policy, so she moved back to Pensacola to write books full-time. She currently resides there with her husband and kids, and frequently can be found plotting on the beach.

Visit S. Usher Evans online at:
http://www.susherevans.com/

www.ingramcontent.com/pod-product-compliance
Lightning Source LLC
Chambersburg PA
CBHW050803190726
48285CB00005B/1780